MASTERING THE ART OF

TIME
MANAGEMENT

MASTERING THE ART OF TIME MANAGEMENT
Highest Use of Your Time to Achieve Your Highest Potential
By Tejgyan Global Foundation

Copyright © Tejgyan Global Foundation
All Rights Reserved 2017

Tejgyan Global Foundation is a charitable organization
with its headquarters in Pune, India.

Published by WOW Publishings Pvt. Ltd., India

First edition published in December 2017
First Reprint published in December 2019

Copyrights are reserved with Tejgyan Global Foundation and publishing rights are vested exclusively with WOW Publishings Pvt. Ltd. This book is sold subject to the condition that it shall not by way of trade or otherwise, be lent, resold, hired out, or otherwise circulated without the publisher's prior written consent in any form of binding or cover other than that in which it is published and without a similar condition including this condition being imposed on the subsequent purchaser and without limiting the rights under copyright reserved above, no part of this publication may be reproduced, stored in or introduced into a retrieval system, or transmitted, in any form, or by any means, electronic, mechanical, photocopying, recording or otherwise, without the prior written permission of both the copyright owner and the above-mentioned publisher of this book. Any person who does any unauthorized act in relation to this publication may be liable to criminal prosecution and civil claims for damages.

Contents

Preface: Become Time-Rich   v

Section I: HOW TO AVOID BEING TIME-POOR

1. Get Tuned With Time   2
2. Recognize Where and How You Are Wasting Time   7
3. How Are You Spending Your Precious Wealth of Time?   13

Section II: PRINCIPLES FOR BECOMING TIME-RICH

4. The 80/20 Principle   20
5. How to Make the Most of the 80/20 Principle   26
6. The Principle of Prioritizing   31
7. The Principle of Setting Time Limits   39

Section III: TIME AND TASK MANAGEMENT

8. Tools to Save Time   48
9. Freedom from the Mental Burden of Work   59
10. Result Producing System   66
11. Goal Management System   78

12.	Enhance Your Energy and Save Time	90
13.	Work is Never Completed by Giving Excuses	95
14.	Give Time for Incomplete Work	104

Section IV: SMALL SAVINGS OF TIME

15.	A Little Time Can Benefit Multiple Tasks	112
16.	The Two-Minutes Technique	118

Section V: HUGE SAVINGS OF TIME

17.	Delegate Tasks and Save Time	124
18.	Save Time with the Power of Your Thoughts	133
19.	Say "No" and Save Your Time	142

Section VI: RIGHT INVESTMENT OF THE WEALTH OF TIME

20.	Save Time and Invest It	148
21.	Get Hi-Tech	157
22.	Make Decisions at the Right Time	162
23.	Utilize the Small Amounts of Time	169
24.	Time to Meditate in Solitude	173

BONUS CHAPTER

Beliefs About Time	180

Preface

BECOME TIME-RICH

*"What is it that I do regularly,
which I can totally discontinue or delegate to someone else?"
Ask yourself this question and find the time to read this book.*

You can't hoard it. You can't speed it up or slow it down. It's your most precious resource, yet it can also be your most frightening nemesis. It's something you can't dispose of but you never seem to have enough of it.

That's *time*. While this sounds like a snappy riddle, it is nothing but the truth. Every generation feels as if it is shackled by time. Perhaps, though, in no other era have the constraints of time been so binding as in our present times.

And perhaps this issue has never been so ironic. The many electronic devices we have at our fingertips and our near instant means of communications, emails, texts, and social media outlets were meant to provide us with more time—more leisure time, more time with family, and more vacation time. Instead, it appears that far too many of us have become enslaved to these electronic marvels. Tethered twenty-four hours a day to our devices, many of us are expected to answer emails and text messages regardless of whether we are on the clock or at home.

If that weren't enough, people seem to be running a race to become "rich," rich in the possession of money and luxuries. Yet they completely ignore the idea of earning first the wealth of time. You can find many so-called strategy experts—ranging from professional financial managers to family members and even virtual strangers—who can tell you how and where to invest your money, and where you can receive the best returns on your investment. This advice is ubiquitous. You'll find no dearth of individuals who will tell you how to take 100 rupees (or dollars or any other form of currency) and multiply it.

But consider this: 100 rupees is the same value for you as for your neighbor. It's the same value whether you are a teacher or a venture capitalist. And when someone makes 20 percent on this money, the 20 rupees are the same value for everyone. But here's the crux of the problem. One hour of your time is not necessarily equal to one hour of your neighbor, your physician, or the CEO of a multi-million-dollar corporation. Consider this: an hour of time for a university student and that of their professor aren't worth the same. A student, for example, who "invests" his hour in studying, benefits himself. His professor, let's say, invests an hour of his time in teaching a class of 60 students. That investment of a mere hour benefits 60 students. So, if the professor would be unable to invest that hour of teaching for whatever reason, the associated loss is actually 60 hours. Why? Because the advice and instruction the students could have experienced are also lost.

Let's consider another example. The owner of a company can value an hour of his time at one thousand hours, since he has a thousand employees depending on his actions. Likewise, think about the value of an hour for the prime minister of a country. It's worth many more thousands of hours, depending on the size of the population of the country.

It's obvious when you view the issue from this perspective that every person's yardstick to measure the investment of time is unique to them. It's why there are no time-investment counselors who can advise you, with accuracy at least, on how you should invest your time.

Ultimately, this then puts the understanding of the value of your time squarely on your shoulders. It also means that you alone can help yourself to become "rich" when it comes to time.

This is where mastering the art of time management comes in. You probably already have some idea of what time management is and its importance. Though, there may be a few lingering questions in your mind: "Should *I* learn how to manage my time better? What would I gain by becoming proficient in time management?"

If you have ever asked yourself these questions, then it's no surprise you have an interest in this book. Learning how to manage time properly is probably the single most important thing you can do to improve your odds at getting ahead at work and to make more time for your family and personal life as well as spiritual growth.

Although you have a general understanding of time management, you may or may not have full knowledge of what it really encompasses. And until you learn that, you will never quite understand how to master your time. Once you gain a fuller understanding of this important productivity tool, there will be no more doubt in your mind. You will become an eager life-long student of time management, ready to master its secrets.

Time management, generally speaking, helps to improve the performance and quality of your daily tasks, whether at work or at home. Let's face it, the quality of your work impacts your professional reputation. When you master time management, you will be able to improve the quality of your tasks. Your capacity to accomplish your work load could very well be vastly improved. Not only that, but you will find that you procrastinate less or perhaps not at all.

When you employ time management techniques regularly, you will find it easier than ever before to steadily advance in the direction of your goals. And you will have the privilege of experiencing the pleasure of achievement.

But that's only the tip of the iceberg. Using these techniques successfully will also give you the confidence to complete every project that you begin. You can not only complete them on time, but also do so nearly error-free, which in the long run saves you time from doing them again. Then, of course, in due course, you'll discover that you have grown to be reliable and trustworthy in the eyes of others.

Then there are those bonuses that come along with being a master of time: more moments with your family, less stress in your life, better health… You probably have many more reasons to save time and improve your productivity. Once you are able to think of all the ways in which saving time will free you up to do things you have always dreamed of, then you will certainly be inspired to become "time-rich."

Now that you have come to know about a few of the benefits of time management, you'll need to know a bit more about this book. First, you will notice that it has been divided into 24 chapters. These chapters will give you the essential insights on investing and planning your time. If you are faced with a shortage of time to read this book, there are some ways to work around that as well. For example, instead of dedicating several hours a day to read, you can easily get the same insights simply by reading for only one hour a day.

Take one hour to read one chapter, digest it, and plan how you are going to implement it. If you choose this option, you can read 24 chapters in a mere 24 hours. In that amount of time, you will have learned the fine art of time investment in just the equivalent of one day.

Additionally, this book is designed to facilitate easy and direct access to a specific section of the book. This means you can open the section you want to read by looking at the side of the book.

Along your journey through this book, you'll notice valuable time management tips scattered across various parts. Go ahead and give them a try. You will master your time by using these vital tips.

Another feature of the book that we hope will help you is that each chapter begins with a few important lines. You may jot these words on paper and stick it someplace where you can see it easily and daily. These words will certainly serve as your personal daily inspiration as well as help in instilling in you a keen awareness of time.

Keep a marker pen or your mobile phone nearby while you read. You can mark or take pictures or note down some of the more important lines that you want to remember and tips you would like to implement.

Sirshree, the author of the bestseller *The Source* and founder of Tej Gyan Foundation says, "You are on Earth on a short visit. Though you are beyond time, make the best use of time to fulfil the purpose of this short visit. Only the highest use of your time will help you in achieving your highest potential." The 24 chapters in this book are a reminder of the fixed 24 hours each one of us gets every day. May you conquer these 24 hours and master time, a dimension of this world, so that you can grow spiritually to realize the dimensions beyond this world.

SECTION I

HOW TO AVOID BEING TIME-POOR

ONE

GET TUNED WITH TIME

How to become time-rich

*Time can become your enemy
if you don't make it your friend.*

Every one of us would like to be wealthy. We usually associate wealth with money and most of us also say health is wealth. However, time is the greatest treasure you can have. After all, life is made up of time. Hence, it is important to become time-rich. But what does this term mean?

To become rich in time means you align, sync, or tune yourself with the flow of time.

When you do this, you'll quickly discover that Nature is more than willing, even eager, to reveal its magnificent secrets to you. All you need to do is attune yourself with Nature. Think of this as "walking hand-in-hand" with Nature. In the same way, if you learn how to adapt and attune yourself with time, you can then discover the secrets of time and become prosperous in terms of time.

Think about your favorite song. It possesses a certain rhythm that

ONE

you can easily sync yourself with. In much the same way, time has a specific rhythm as well. Only when you learn the secrets to matching with the beat of time and practice operating with its rhythm will you ever become time-rich, even time-wealthy.

While this sounds quite reasonable, you may find that it's easier said than done. And you may be surprised to learn the first essential step you take to walking with the rhythm of time is quite surprising and even counterintuitive. At least at first glance.

One of the aspects that complicates this attuning to its rhythm is the fact that every hour has its own individual set of beats. That's right. No two hours in your day may have the same rhythm. If the beats change hourly, then you'll need a tool to help you navigate these beats.

Think of what some individuals call the "tempo of time." The clock in your living room strikes 1:01, then 2:02, 3:03, and on and on it goes. The key to adopting this tempo of time as your own is to synchronize yourself with this steady rhythm. And this can be accomplished, believe it or not, to "save" two minutes out of each of these hours for yourself.

What good is a measly two minutes, one may ask. What can you do in two minutes?

Simply by claiming these two minutes, you can not only transform your entire day but also make stunning changes in your life as well.

Here's all you need to do:

Pull out two minutes from each and every hour in your day, right from the time you wake up. As soon as it strikes 8:08, 9:09, 10:10, and so on, close your eyes for two minutes. Think about how you've spent the preceding hour and what you'd like to do to make the best investment in the next hour.

As simple as that you are performing a self-analysis of your time. And because of this, you will discover that you are more alert to what lies ahead and how you handle it, as well as how you can achieve more productivity in the hour that follows.

In effect, you are conducting what's often referred to as a "self-observation." It's one of the most beneficial exercises you can undertake. If you are working to improve yourself and hone all the good qualities within you, this is the most important activity you can perform. By doing this, you will soon be able to see the opportunities in the past hour that you could have used to improve. You will also recognize which opportunities you seized and which you passed on.

This is also a useful tool if you want to eliminate negative qualities and practices from your life. For example, anger. Scan your actions in the past hour and review the number of times you got angry. Also, be sure to examine the number of times you successfully avoided anger or channeled it properly. Once you have taken note of that, then you are in a position to raise your consciousness about the potential triggers of anger and how to handle them in the next hour.

Want to Achieve Spiritual Growth?

This technique is particularly useful if you wish to achieve spiritual growth. There are questions you can ask. "What are the beliefs about myself with which I was operating in the previous hour? How would I do differently in the following hour? Was I considering myself to be a limited individual in the last one hour? How can I be unlimited in the following hour?" In this way, you can cultivate an alertness throughout the day.

Perhaps your desire is to heighten your decision-making abilities. In this case, the questions you may ask as you review the previous hour would be in the vein of: How many times was I able to make decisions independently in the past hour? How many decisions I made with the help of my co-workers or family members?" After analyzing this, you can decide to consciously take decisions on your own in the upcoming hour. This goes a long way in keeping you sharp and observant in the next hour and to develop your decision-making ability.

What does all this mean? It indicates that regardless of what you may think at this moment, you do have an option to choose about whether you stay vigilant throughout the day. It's all too easy to start the day with the best of intentions. But you know what happens as the day wears on. You are so involved in the details of the day that one hour turns into two, and before you know, your resolution to stay aware all day has somehow dissipated, and you can't even pinpoint when your attentiveness waned.

But with this method, not only can you choose to stay vigilant, but you can work at effectively developing a certain facet of yourself or eliminating an unwanted one.

This is a great idea; you may be thinking. *But, how can I implement it?* Depending on when you wake up each morning, you can start using this powerful tool simply by setting a buzzer to remind yourself every hour. Many folks simply use their mobile for this by setting the alarms for, say 7:07, 8:08, 9:09, and so on. From the time you awaken in the morning till you retire for the night, keep the alarms, egg timers, or whatever you're using, to implement this idea.

ONE

You may say, why not 7:00, 8:00, etc. instead of 7:07, 8:08…? That's because, generally saying that they will do it every hour has not proven to be helpful to many people. Hence, a unique time-set is being recommended. What you should know is that in Tej Gyan Foundation, thousands of people have reported that when they began practicing this time-tuned self-investigation at 7:07, 8:08, etc., it was much easier for them to remember to do it.

Additionally, these particular times are being suggested because they have a rhythm about them. Everything in nature works in a rhythm. By following these rhythmic times, you will start getting tuned to the rhythm of nature as well as time. It also helps you to develop discipline over your body-mind. What's wonderful is that after a few months of vigorous practice, it will become a part of your auto-system. That means it will become automatic for you and you won't have to put in much effort. Thereafter, even other activities will start happening on time, because you are tuned with time.

Think of it. By merely investing two minutes out of every hour gives you the potential to win a lottery equivalent to two million.

Congratulations! Just imagine, you can win a lottery of time every hour and become rich in the wealth of time.

> *The bad news is time flies.*
> *The good news is you're the pilot.*
>
> – Michael Altshuler

RECOGNIZE WHERE AND HOW YOU'RE WASTING TIME

Kill your time killers

Mourning over lost time only results in more lost time. Instead prepare yourself and work harder for the next trial you face.

Let's read a small story that will help us realize in what pursuits should we be spending our precious time on Earth.

> A young man was struck by the beauty of a young woman who was an accomplished dancer. He instantly fell for her. Determined to marry her, he told his father of his decision. His father, though, refused to give his blessing for the marriage. Nevertheless, his son persisted, and finally persuaded his father to relent and allow him to marry her.
>
> Excited and filled with hope and anticipation, this young man then met with the young woman's father. He formally asked for his daughter's hand in marriage. The girl's father

ONE

too was reluctant about the marriage, hence he said he could allow the marriage only on one condition: that his future son-in-law study to be a dancer as well. He told the young man it was the custom in their community that an artist must marry another artist. The young man remained undeterred. He had a burning desire in his heart to marry her. If he were required to become a dancer himself, so be it.

The young man informed his father of the stipulations, who was put off and withdrew his approval. But his son again persisted. The father saw that his boy would not take no for an answer, as he was blind in love and was willing to do whatever it took to marry the girl. Finally, he relented to his son's stubbornness. The young man immediately started taking lessons and within six months he showed an outstanding proficiency at his newly honed talent.

While he considered himself quite good, according to the custom of his future in-law's community, there was only one way to be declared proficient. He must dance before the king. If the king did not applaud his performance, then he was not proficient and, of course, would be unable to marry the girl.

The king was informed and after receiving his permission, a dance recital was organized. The king knew that if he applauded, this young man would then be able to marry the love of his life. There sat the king on the day of the recital, front and center. The king took one look at the young woman who was the object of this man's love, and could understand his persistence in learning to dance. But the king also realized at that moment that he, himself, had

ONE

fallen in love with her at first sight and decided that he wanted to marry her.

You can certainly see what the problem had become. The young man had, in a relatively short period, devoted a great deal of time and energy in ensuring that he would present an amazing performance, and he succeeded. But the king, purposely withheld his applause, even though every other person in attendance clapped and cheered wildly.

Everyone involved in this event had their own perspective about it, including the young man himself, his father, the girl, her father, and the king, to name just a few. The king decided he wanted to make the dance more difficult for this young man. The king's goal? To make the dance challenge impossible to win. He was expecting that the young man would fall to his defeat. He ordered a stage constructed that would literally dangle in the air. The king felt certain it would take a herculean effort for the dancer to present his best from this type of platform.

After the stage was built, a recital was organized once again, and the young man danced passionately once more. After all, he was consumed to the point of obsession with the desire to marry the girl of his dreams. His incredible performance again stunned the audience. How could he possibly dance on a stage suspended in the air? The young man impressed everyone, except the one person he needed to—the king. The king, still driven by his own personal agenda, refused to applaud.

But then something quite remarkable occurred. As the

ONE

young man danced high on this platform, he had a bird's eye view of the members of the audience. His attention, though, was drawn towards one man in particular: the craftsman who had designed the stage.

That man was in complete bliss and at peace with himself. He was detached from everything around him, even though he was amidst a large crowd. People were praising him for his stunning creation. The king's maids were serving him the best of delicacies. They were even more beautiful than the woman he loved and were fawning all over him. But from what the young man could detect, the craftsman was untouched by all of this. His attention was focused on the stage and he looked truly happy and fulfilled by his creation.

This scene struck a chord in the dancer, opening his eyes to the futility of his own efforts, dancing high on a platform. "What am I doing? Is this really meaningful for my life?"

These questions took hold of him. He felt, "I am wasting my time and energy in vain. My dream was never to become a dancer. I'm doing all of this not out of love, but obsession. Instead of being consumed by an obsession, I need to let go of it and aspire toward higher goals of life." Once he realized this, he squandered no more time with dancing on the suspended stage. He jumped off and bowed to the king, accepting his defeat. He then walked off the venue.

What we can understand from this parable is that when the young man saw the craftsman, he realized his mistake. He could finally see clearly that he had put his whole life at stake for fulfilling an obsession. Instead, if he would have invested his time and energy toward attaining the ultimate purpose of his life (for which he had a fervent thirst), his life would have become truly meaningful.

The set designer, by contrast, was well aware of his purpose and totally focused on it, unaffected by any distractions. He symbolizes an individual who is filled with a passionate zeal to achieve his goal, regardless of what others may say about him or want from him.

The designer took on a new goal and a new challenge when he envisioned the suspended stage and then worked towards making it a reality. The adulation and everything else was a by-product. In the same way, when you have a clear objective and goal, and work toward it with perseverance, you'll discover that everything else will be attracted to you on its own.

Not only that, but the bliss the set designer enjoyed simply by reveling in his own creativity overpowered any distractions like the lovely maids that were at his beck and call. His attention, you see, was not directed at the distractions. Rather, with laser-like vision, he drilled a hole through the distractions and focused only on the manifestation of his vision.

On looking at the craftsman, the dancer realized he too had a powerful goal for his life. He understood that he was wasting his talents, time, and energy in the pursuit of sensual pleasures. Instead, he should put his time to the highest use.

Once he understood this, he became rich with respect to time; he became time-rich. He then invested that very time in comprehending and fulfilling the ultimate purpose of his life.

This story implores us to take a second look at how we possibly could be wasting our time and energy in any number of myriad ways while carrying out our daily activities, thereby becoming impoverished

ONE

when it comes to time. The activities that waste our time are called "time killers." If you truly desire to not only be "time-rich" and to achieve your most sought after desires, then eliminating these time killers is imperative.

The only way you can clearly see where your time killers wait in ambush for you, is to become keenly observant throughout the day. With awareness, you will realize the futility of some of the activities you indulge in. Just as the dancer realized how his dancing efforts were in vain. If you stay alert all day, the incidents that suck your valuable time will pop out before you at any moment.

This requires effort, determination, and vigilance. You must be cognizant from when you first wake up in the morning till when you fall asleep at night. The question that will be in your head is: "What is it that I do all day?" Consciously observe everything that you do throughout the day. As soon as you realize that some of your activities are totally unnecessary and don't promote your goal or passion, you will automatically get rid of those activities.

It is in this way that you will become wealthy in terms of time and benefit from every moment of your day.

This is easier with those who have a goal in life. If you don't have a goal, you can read books that can help you find your goal—a goal that will help you grow externally as well as internally. You can then use your precious time to achieve that goal.

> *You can't make up for lost time.*
> *You can only do better in the future.*
>
> – Ashley Ormon

HOW ARE YOU SPENDING YOUR PRECIOUS WEALTH OF TIME?

Be aware of your time investments and beliefs

*Go to sleep with gratitude at night.
A good night's sleep saves you time the next day.*

Yay!! Finally, the day has arrived. You have been preparing for this event for a while and you are excited. It's a one-day cricket match. You have got everything lined up. In fact, you went to great lengths to organize this. You have not only spent your time and your energy, those tickets weren't cheap either, so you've got some money invested as well.

Since cricket is such an absorbing sport, you didn't realize how much you had already spent, not only in money, but in your other resources as well. But when you stopped and totaled it up, you were stunned at how much it was.

This example of a cricket match is meant to illustrate the time management of a person who only has a spectator interest in the sport. If you are working toward becoming a professional cricketer

ONE

or if you are connected with cricket activities, you'd of course have a different perspective. In that case, it could be a valuable investment for your future.

When you stop to think how much of your resources were "invested" in this "excursion" is when you take a step back and look very carefully at the details. You can then ask the following 4 questions:

1. How does this cricket match contribute to my life?
2. If I didn't watch it, what difference would it make in my life?
3. What would I lose if I didn't watch it? What would I gain if I did?
4. Instead, could I have invested this time in something more important?

By answering these questions honestly, you can begin to understand the true amount of time, energy, and money you have invested in this event. In the same vein, if you carefully thought through these questions in all the various areas of your life, you will have a much clearer picture of where your wealth of time is being frittered away. The following groups of questions are typical of some of the questions that could be asked by most people.

A. *At the physical plane*

1. Does overeating benefit my body?
2. How long does my sense of taste hold on to impressions from excess food?
3. How much time and energy is wasted to digest this excess food?

4. How has watching TV shows benefited me?

5. Considering the benefits, how much time should I allot to such activities?

6. Have I benefited in any way by chatting or gossiping?

7. Could I possibly invest this time in exercising instead?

B. **At the mental plane**

1. How has harboring negative thoughts and emotions like fear, envy, ego, anger, remorse helped me so far?

2. How does getting carried away by negative emotions serve me?

3. Could I invest this time and energy in contemplation or prayer?

C. **At the social plane**

1. What have I gained till date from going to parties?

2. Is the time I have invested proportionate with what I have gained? Have I invested too much time in it?

3. Could I have devoted this time to my family or toward developing a new skill?

D. **At the financial plane**

1. What have I gained so far by spending money simply to show off?

2. In the process of competing with others, how much money have I squandered?

3. Could I have used this money in a better way?

E. *On the spiritual level*

1. Due to the distractions and excuses of the mind, how long have I avoided practicing meditation?

2. What have I benefited by believing or agreeing with my mind?

3. Instead of spending time and energy in being absorbed in frivolous thoughts of the mind, could I utilize them instead for sitting in meditation or listening to spiritual discourses?

When you carefully scrutinize these little activities, you can discover the amount of time you are wasting. Armed with this information, you can then begin to curb these activities. In turn, you can rid yourself of what can amount to large chunks of wasted time.

Beliefs about time

Very often, people form and act on certain beliefs regarding time management that aren't actually based on proven facts. These beliefs are derived popular myths. Instead of gaining time, people are actually losing considerable time by getting entangled in them. The sooner you understand the futility of these false pretenses, the faster you begin saving your time. As you read through the following list of beliefs, honestly check if you too harbor these beliefs.

Belief 1: You can control and hoard time.

Belief 2: Time management is the art of accomplishing maximum work in the least possible time.

Belief 3: Being engaged on the telephone, sudden visitors, and meetings are major time killers.

Belief 4: You should not undertake another task if you already have one in hand. You must be engaged only in completing the first job. In other words, you should not multitask. This is the most effective method of working.

Belief 5: We should create separate planners for office work and home.

Belief 6: I am the only person who can accomplish a particular job efficiently and quickly; no one else can. Entrusting the work to someone else will only result in time being wasted.

Belief 7: I must complete all the jobs entrusted to me by everyone. I must meet the expectations of all and ensure everyone is happy.

Belief 8: Just making a list of all my tasks is time management.

Belief 9: No matter how much you try to plan your time, an emergency always pops up thwarting all of your plans. Then, why should I even try to manage my time?

Belief 10: If I work hard enough, I can complete all my tasks.

Belief 11: Why should I waste time trying to manage time when I don't have the time to manage time?

(You can read the reality behind each of these beliefs on Pg 180.)

Are these some of the beliefs that are stuck in your mind? You are unable to accomplish so many things due to these beliefs. Simply

ONE

believing these statements is and of itself a waste of your valuable time. This is not easily realized by most of us.

The good news is that realizing these beliefs as pointless is the first step in getting rid of them on the path of mastering your time.

Also, after finishing any activity, ask yourself the four questions presented in the beginning part of this chapter. By doing so, you will become conscious of the futility of some of your activities. You would then be ready to give them up and find some free time for yourself. You can make good use of this time and become time-rich. You will be delighted, even amazed, to be able to complete your important tasks thoroughly instead of struggling through the day feeling as if you haven't given your tasks the time they deserve. But there is an even bigger benefit to all of this. By becoming time-rich, you can give time to better your health, increase your income, strengthen your relationships, and also make time for your spiritual growth.

*Let our advance worrying
become advance thinking and planning.*

– Winston Churchill

SECTION 11

PRINCIPLES FOR BECOMING TIME-RICH

TWO

THE 80/20 PRINCIPLE

The method of focusing on important tasks

Those who tackle their tasks right from the first day of the week, gain inner strength and confidence that transform them forever.

If you want to be time-rich, then your first lesson is to learn what the 80/20 Principle is and how you can ensure it works in your favor, today and every day. Haven't heard about this handy rule of thumb? You'll discover that this rule can change the way you approach not only your job but your personal life as well.

When talking about this well-known rule in time management, it means 80% of your energy should be invested in tasks which will contribute to the development of your home, family, profession, yourself, and society at large.

But, more often than not, many individuals invest 80% of their energy in activities that make them feel, at the end of the day, that only 20% of their tasks were accomplished. *We must actually carry out those 20% of our activities that can genuinely have 80% result.*

Your energies must be invested only in those 20% critical tasks which will provide you 80% of satisfaction, or else at the end of the day, after constant expenditure of energy, you won't feel satisfied. Those individuals who feel content and can honestly say that they have experienced a rewarding day are those who complete their 20% vital tasks. The key to achieving this, though, is to learn what projects or responsibilities fall into the critical or vital 20% zone. This is done by reviewing all the activities of the day. Then, you need to ask yourself, "In what jobs am I investing my energies?"

To truly understand this analysis, it's best to review the following examples.

> Darren Hardy, an American author, publisher, CEO, and an advisor, was a busy man. He was occupied all day long, like most people. He realized that telephone conversations, emails, deadlines, and other daily duties leave him with no time for anything else. He discovered that while he was indeed a very busy man, yet he knew that his mistake was that he spent most of his time in not-very-productive ways.
>
> He decided he needed to break free from his being that busy every single day. The way to do this, he thought, was simply to find ways to reduce his daily activities. Instead of spinning his wheels on seemingly unimportant, extraneous activities, he would focus his efforts only on those crucial projects from his to-do list that would promulgate his agenda and work toward his goals.
>
> After he took some time to rearrange the order of his tasks, he found a solution to his busy day and made his time yield more profits.

TWO

This is where the 80/20 principle proved useful to Hardy. According to this principle, you focus your energies on those 20% tasks that will work towards the accomplishment of 80% of your goals. By focusing on a mere 20% of his tasks, he actually did achieve 80% of his goals. As a result, he was able to make his life more satisfying and he became time-rich.

The 80/20 principle helps you save time by making you concentrate your energies only on important activities. It teaches you to focus on those 20% of your tasks that give you the maximum results—80% of the results. According to this principle, every task can be broken down in an 80/20 ratio. This means that every activity has 20% which is vital, that absolutely needs to be completed. The rest of the activity—up to 80% to be precise—is less important. You will fully understand this after reviewing a few examples.

1. A homemaker uses salt while cooking. It's a mere 20% of the spices in her recipe. But if the remaining 80% of the ingredients were added and cooked without that salt, the food would remain tasteless and would not be as tasty and satisfying.

2. Similarly, when we talk about friends and relatives, it's only 20% of them who contribute to 80% of contentment in your life. You are not nearly as close to the other 80%. In fact, you may even be tempted to consider them as acquaintances. They don't provide you with the essential support and love in your life. They make only a 20% difference to your life.

3. You can even extend this principle to items like a wedding invitation. What is the 20% of the important information?

The date, time, and venue of the wedding and reception. But the name of the relatives of the bride and groom, their business, and other information comprise 80% of the card, which is not of much interest to guests. Think about it this way: that 80% won't ensure that you make it to the wedding on the right day, time, and place.

As you can see, if you decide to implement this principle, you'll need to clearly identify the vital 20% tasks of your day, which contribute to 80% of effective results. If this 20% is not accomplished, by the way, it will cause complications in your life.

How do you analyze your activities and projects, so you can determine their vital 20%? The first thing you need to understand is that the most important component of any task at hand, is the benefit or success it provides you. If the activity doesn't benefit you or gets you any closer to your goals, then what's the point of doing it? For example, suppose your company shows great sales numbers, but the benefits like financial profit, goodwill of clients, and customer trust are very low, then devoting your time in gaining even greater numbers of sales is of no use. Hence, choose only those activities which will provide the said benefits. These constitute your 20% vital tasks.

When you focus your entire energy on these 20% tasks from your daily list, then 80% of the results are assured. For example, does physical exercise constitute 20% of your daily tasks or the 80%? If it's 20%, then you'll definitely invest your time in an exercise program. You're aware that exercise or yoga and proper diet constitute the vital 20% that leads to 80% results: good health. Instead of waiting for your doctor to give you this advice, it would be helpful to begin to exercise right away. Learn to identify the vital 20% of your life!

Whenever you feel that your time is being wasted, remind yourself about the 20% vital tasks that you need to pay attention to. Making the most effective use of your time means identifying, defining, and focusing on the 20% essential tasks of your day.

Mentioned below are some questions for self-analysis, to assess whether you are using your time effectively. If your answer is "yes" to the questions given below, you might be trapped in the least consequential 80% of your daily tasks.

- Do you spend your time in doing things that have nothing to do with you but have been entrusted to you by others?

    Yes/No

- Are you constantly completing tasks that are urgent but don't align with your goal?

    Yes/No

- Are you investing your time in activities that you're not skilled or proficient at?

    Yes/No

- Do you invest more than the pre-determined time in all of your activities?

    Yes/No

- Do you frequently complain of not having enough time or being bogged down with too many tasks at the same time?

    Yes/No

Next, analyze the questions below. If your answer is "yes" to these, it indicates that you're focused on the important 20% tasks in your day which yield 80% success.

- Are you generally engaged in activities that contribute to the achievement of your life's goal?

    Yes/ No

- Are you engaged in the activities you've always wanted to do and you enjoy doing?

    Yes/ No

- Are you investing your time in tasks you don't find enjoyable but are necessary for your future success?

    Yes/ No

- Have you delegated the jobs that you don't particularly like or aren't proficient at to those who are skilled at them?

    Yes/ No

From the questions above, you can get a fair idea as to where you have been investing your time: in 20% important activities or 80% unimportant activities. Using this information, you can now focus your energy only on the 20% vital tasks.

If you wish to bring about change in the world, there's one task that's 20% but provides 80% results—which is prayer. Invest your time in praying for those 20% people of the world—the leaders of the world—who, if they underwent change within, can change the world for the better.

In this way, you can see that the 80/20 principle can work in every area of your life.

> *It is not enough to be busy; so are ants!*
> *The question is: What are we busy about?*
>
> – Henry David Thoreau

TWO

5

HOW TO MAKE THE MOST OF THE 80/20 PRINCIPLE

Application in every aspect of life

> *Prepare your schedule
> and then live spontaneously.*

It's one thing to understand what the 80/20 rule is, but quite another to confidently say you can apply it to your life so you can truly save time, effort, and energy. Are you ready to take your newly garnered knowledge to the next level, to ensure you get the most out of your day?

Until you do this, you may be missing the mark in soaring to the next level of success. In order to make the most of this amazing rule, you will need to know how to apply it in all the different areas of your life. In doing so, you'll be asking yourself many of the following questions.

At the physical level:

What are the 20% important tasks at the physical level, which if you give your time to, then rest of the activities will automatically get done?

Most individuals, as well as time management experts, agree that the most important activity has to be that of gaining and maintaining good health. It may be a cliché, but it's true that if you don't have your health, you have nothing. You have probably already noticed the marvelous side effects of maintaining and improving your health. When you purposely and regularly invest time working on this goal, then your body is energized and you'll find how much more quickly you will be zipping through all of your activities all day long.

So, what's involved in maintaining a healthy body? Of course, you'll want to set your exercise schedule to target your specific physical needs. You'll also want to do it at a time during the day when you believe it will do the most good. This may mean that you may have to adjust the times you perform your regime in order to see when it does you the most good.

In general, there are three components of a program—any program—to maintain a healthy body: daily exercise, *pranayama*, and the right diet. Invest a part of your time in these three activities and you will discover how much it increases your productivity and the ease with which you carry out the rest of the 80% tasks.

At the mental level:

Along with a healthy body, a healthy mind is essential to efficient time management. The adverse effects of a low state of mind can eventually and undeniably take its toll on your body. You know what that looks like. We've all seen at least one friend mired in a problem, and while he's struggling with it, you can tell something is wrong within him, even if he doesn't confide in you. You can read it on his face, in his body language, and by any number of other traits he displays.

On the other hand, you can immediately spot someone who has a healthy mind. In some cases, you can tell simply by listening to the tone of their voice. So, it's obvious that the 20% you need to pay attention to involves keeping your mind stress-free and happy.

What will help you most to do so is, to organize and manage your activities in the best manner. If you give 20% of your time in organizing your tasks in the most effective way, that will yield 80% results. This will relieve the stress in your mind and keep you in high spirits. Many powerful time and task management techniques are presented further in this book.

At the social level:

Your relationships with others throughout the day—from your supervisors to clients to your family—are referred to as your social level. You will notice that the important 20% of your relationships when managed well will automatically improve and harmonize the remaining 80%.

So, the question you must ask yourself is this: "What are those relationships that are very important to me? When those are managed well, then the rest will automatically be taken care of?" Once you can answer that, you are then set to focus on 20% of your relationships. This saves you a lot of time and energy. But more than that, you'll be experiencing an amazing improvement in your interactions with your closest and most cherished friends and family.

At the economic level:

In order to use the 80/20 rule to increase your economic well-being, review your account and other areas of your financial life in order to see what are the jobs or activities you can focus on that will lead to your financial progress. Financial progress does not occur only through earnings but through savings too. Focus on those areas of your life where you can save. Your 20% savings can make your livelihood easier.

At the spiritual level:

Listening to a true spiritual guru's teachings is essential for spiritual growth. If you can invest even one hour a week to stop and listen to the true teachings, it will tremendously help in raising your level of consciousness. This one hour of sincere listening to the truth can take you toward Self Realization.

*In reality, killing time
is only the name for another of the multifarious ways
by which time kills us.*

– Sir Osbert Sitwell

TWO

Smart Tip to Master Your Time

WANT TO SAVE TIME AT YOUR WORKPLACE?

Do your co-workers, colleagues, and others sit in front of your desk, talking idly and whiling away your time? Feeling frustrated about this? Want to regain your time?

The best way to handle this is simply to move the chairs away from the front of your desk. Your "visitors" will feel less comfortable standing and talking to you while you are sitting.

That means people may come and speak for a few moments, but they won't stand talking to you for very long.

Doing this puts an end to needless or futile chatter. People will engage in concise conversation with you, only that much which is actually required. You will be able to salvage a lot of time in this manner.

THE PRINCIPLE OF PRIORITIZING

Make the appropriate choice of tasks

There are at least 10,000 quotations related to "time."
24 are enough to give you guidance.

You know you have a full day of activities that absolutely need to be dealt with in a satisfactory way. You have just finished one task and instead of moving on to the next one, you discover that you're playing a game on your mobile, surfing the net, or carrying on a lengthy telephone conversation with a friend. Before you know it, an hour or two has flown by.

You wonder how you could have possibly allowed this to happen. For one thing, you haven't written down your most important tasks for the day. This, in turn, means your most important activities aren't fully set in your conscious mind.

How can you avoid these time wasters? There's a time and place for such activities, of course, but the middle of the workday isn't it. Simply by writing a list of items that must be completed for the day can make a huge difference in the way you approach the day and how you spend your valuable time.

Once you've written the list, then place it in a location where you are sure to see it all day. You may want to place it on your computer screen, for example. Wherever you decide to place it, it's an effective visual reminder of what you need to do. This list is vital in the process of completing a minimum of 80% of your tasks.

If you have this list on your computer, or even your mobile screen, you'll be far less tempted to surf the web for interesting and entertaining ideas that make no contribution to getting your daily goals completed.

There's another advantage, as well, when you have your list in front and center. Because you can see it at a glance, you won't be wasting time in searching for it. Similarly, you won't be wasting time trying to figure out the next task you should be working on.

But perhaps the emotional satisfaction you receive is the most important reason for doing it. As you tick off each task as being completed, you feel a sense of satisfaction.

Sort tasks according to priority

Even before you make your list of activities, you need to think them through in the order of importance of completing them on this day. For this, you need to sort them according to the priority that they have in your day.

When you create this list, be sure to include all the tasks you have facing you. You'll see in a few moments why this is essential. A few of these tasks will be important. Another few will be urgent. Some of these various activities will be interesting to work on and others you will undoubtedly find monotonous and tedious.

Now, look at these activities from a psychological viewpoint.

It's only human nature to tackle those tasks that are easy and interesting first. We try to ignore and procrastinate in working on those we have less of an interest in. And can you guess what your task list looks like by the end of the day? A large chunk of important duties, which may not be as "fun" or interesting, are untouched and are simply transferred to the next day.

This means that your list should be sorted according to priority. What absolutely must get done today—no excuses—you need to complete those first. So, as you make the list, you prioritize them, and then you can accomplish them in a timely manner. This means, even if you get absolutely nothing else done (an unlikely scenario), you will at the very least have completed the most important ones before the end of the day. Thereby, you receive a healthy bonus: your stress level is greatly reduced. Imagine finishing a day of work and not being anxious about what will happen the following day. There's nothing to worry about because you are up to date with your activities.

To establish priority, use the technique described below. It's called "The A.B.C.D. Technique." As you might have already guessed, this method of prioritizing requires you to divide your duties into four separate sections. The activities are divided according to how vital they are for reaching your goals for that day.

First Category: "A" priority — Important and Urgent

The first category is labeled "A." These tasks are both important and urgent.

The tasks, which are labeled "important," are those that no one but you can follow-through on. They are urgent because they are useless if you wait even until tomorrow to do them. This means you can't ignore or postpone them. They demand your full attention and they demand it as soon as possible. The only way, in fact, that they can be of full benefit to you, is if you accomplish them within the specified time period. A good example of an activity that you'd put in this category, if you were a student, is studying for a test that is scheduled for the following day.

You can see how studying for it after you have taken the test wouldn't be of much use. That's why it is classified as urgent. And it is important because only you can study for the test you're taking. This is a classic example of a duty that can't be delegated.

But you must be observant as you go through your list to complete these tasks labeled as "A." Investing too much time on these will limit your ability to accomplish the others effectively and only boost your stress level.

It's safe to say that nearly all the tasks in category A will be those you can consider to be in a state of emergency and can assume a serious nature. The only way to avoid dealing with too many Category A activities is by working on them diligently while they are still at the "B" level, so they never get to the point of moving into the "A" category.

Accomplishing the tasks in this category is a necessity. Here the most important factor being: completing these activities on time.

Second Category: "B" Priority — Important but Not Urgent

The tasks in this category are definitely important but not urgent. This means that only you can complete these activities; you can't delegate them to anyone else. But you can postpone doing them for a short time, as long as you don't procrastinate and they end up turning into urgent. Hence, it's important to set a deadline for completing these activities, so that you can work a bit on them every day.

If you neglect these for too long, always putting them off, these tasks can at any time move to the A category and cause you stress. For example, a program scheduled to be held two months from today will require you do something on it every day. You don't need to give it much time, but the important thing is that you make a little progress on it daily to avoid it being suddenly sitting in Category A—Important and Urgent—with the potential to stress you out.

If you don't do a small activity on a daily basis toward that goal, you can end up only a few days before the deadline, overwhelmed by the amount of work still not completed. Not planning in such a way can result in a colossal pile-up of tasks to be accomplished in the last few hours just before the program, which can cause a lot of tension and other problems. Therefore, after completing the A tasks from your list, it's crucial to give your attention to the B category.

Accomplishing the tasks in this category requires intelligent use of your discernment and skills as well as your leadership abilities. The most important factor in accomplishing these tasks successfully is that they must always be in your field of attention. Do not allow them to slip from your memory and into the background. At any time, they can all too easily turn into category A tasks.

Third Category: "C" priority — Not Important but Urgent

It is the "urgent" nature of a job that strangulates the accomplishment.

The tasks in this category are urgent but not important. This may sound paradoxical, but you'll see why these activities are classified in this way in a moment.

You'll notice that a lot of your time is spent executing many tasks from this category. The jobs in this category may create the illusion that since they are urgent, they may be important too. That's why you may be already spending too much time working on these, but you had no idea how to spend less time on them. Consequently, you are not able to spare any time for activities that will lead you toward the goal of your life. The truth of the matter is that your time should be invested most heavily in the A and B categories.

You will be surprised to learn that the tasks of the third category, which you spend so much time on, can be delegated to someone else. For example, today is the last date for a particular bill payment. It's not important that you yourself get it done. It can easily be given to someone else. As you prioritize these tasks, you must also establish who can accomplish them, and assign them to those individuals accordingly.

Thus, when dealing with C category tasks, be careful about the time you spend on them or you can totally avoid doing them yourself by delegating them.

Fourth Category: "D" priority — Not Important, Not urgent

The tasks belonging to this category are neither important nor urgent. If we fritter our time away doing any of these, we start becoming careless and irresponsible. These tasks do not bring any change in our life, neither do we get any closer to the achievement of our goals by performing these tasks. Instead, we have clearly wasted our time by spending our efforts working on them.

That may sound harsh but it's the truth. The tasks that don't align with your goals must be avoided as much as possible. Examples of these types of activities include, but are not limited to, attending weddings of distant relatives, playing games on the mobile, surfing the internet unnecessarily, watching television or reading the newspaper excessively.

Carrying out tasks that belong to the fourth category wastes your time and must be completely eliminated from your list.

Now that you understand the four categories, your first step should be to establish time limits for completion of the tasks belonging to the first category. For example, you could set a time limit of 6:00 am – 8:00 am. During this time, you must complete the items in the first category. That means you have to dedicate yourself to working on only these items. You must purposely set aside all items in every other category. To ensure these tasks have your full attention, it would be wise to switch off your mobile and focus single-mindedly on the completion of these tasks. By doing this, they will be completed smoothly and efficiently and most importantly on time.

Once the tasks of the first category have been accomplished, you will be able to give time to other tasks easily and happily.

1ˢᵗ Category – A	2ⁿᵈ Category – B
Important and Urgent Time bound tasks, which you yourself need to complete within a specific time-frame.	**Important but Not Urgent** Tasks that cannot afford to get pushed into the first category. E.g.: Making action plans, executing a job in a new way, conducting meetings.
3ʳᵈ Category – C	4ᵗʰ Category – D
Urgent but Not Important These are tasks that can be delegated to someone else. E.g.: Bill payment, sending messages or emails.	**Not Important, Not Urgent** These tasks don't align with your goals. E.g.: Engaging in entertainment or gossip.

Don't put off until tomorrow what you can do today.

– Benjamin Franklin

THE PRINCIPLE OF SETTING TIME LIMITS

The method of accomplishing jobs in a limited time

Use your time with awareness, so that you can live happily. Get down to work, so that your time is spent meaningfully.

It is, without a doubt, one of the most important laws of time management you may or may not have heard of. That doesn't mean you've not experienced it. We all have. It's either an amazing law or an amazingly frustrating one, depending on how you are using it.

What is it? It's Parkinson's Law and it states: *Work expands so as to fill the time available for its completion.* It was first recognized and succinctly summarized in 1955 by Cyril Northcote Parkinson.

How does it work? The length of time a given activity takes to complete is dependent on the amount of time you have to finish it. In other words, suppose you have been assigned a project at work and given two months to finish it. The odds are that you will finish it in two months' time. If, though, you're handed the same project with only a month's deadline, the chances are you would then finish it in a month.

In essence, the amount of work involved in the project had expanded in the first example to fill in the time that it was expected to be complete. It's extremely important, if you are serious about getting a grip on your time management skills, that you understand this vital relationship between time and work.

It might be a bit easier to understand by taking a look at a one-day cricket match. One team chases the score established by the other team. It doesn't matter if the score is 225 runs in a 50-over match or if it's 325 runs. Regardless of the goal, it's achieved only in the last 5-6 overs most of the times.

Similarly, a person with a large goal to accomplish will be sure to make efficient use of his time, especially if it's limited. Another person, let's say, with a smaller goal but the same deadline, is utilizing only a small amount of time and in the process much of his time may be wasted.

You may have already been witness to these types of situations. For example, in the days approaching a wedding, there is an abundance of activities to finish within a fixed deadline. There's no pushing back the date of a wedding when the invitations have gone out, the reception hall has been rented, and all the food has been ordered.

Imagine this same planning but without a fixed deadline. You are liable to find that it takes months just to decide on a caterer or the types of flowers and decoration.

The point is simply this: you are able to complete a specific job much more quickly if your goal is crystal clear and you set a fixed time limit for its completion—what some people call a "drop-dead deadline." This means there is absolutely no excuse for completing it a day or even ten minutes late.

If Parkinson's Law is correct, then you can complete a larger amount of work in less time or in a longer period of time as well. It all depends on the deadline.

This seems to align quite nicely with the adage: If you need to delegate a task, assign it to a person who is already busy, so it can be achieved in a short period of time. But if the same job is given to a person who is unsuitable for it, they will complete your work over a long period, maybe many more days than you had anticipated.

Knowing that Parkinson's Law exists and exactly how it works, it can work to your advantage in setting your time management goals. To be able to work within the confines of this law, you first need to develop the ability to define and limit time. You need to instill within yourself the habit of creating time limits for the completion of all of your tasks.

Very often, when you are about to embrace an activity, you truly don't have any idea of the length of time it will take to complete. When this occurs, you usually finish it according to your state of mind at that time and the environment you are in. When you do this, you could very well be taking a month to finish a project that may need only a week of your time.

It seems only logical then that at the outset of a project, establish a specific date and time in which to finish it. Make it a "time-bound" task instead of an open-ended, potentially "timeless" task B activity which can be completed in its own sweet time. By assigning it a deadline, you can help yourself in making sure the activity is indeed completed as soon as possible. A deadline gives you the motivation to do it within the time frame.

Here is a good example of what we're talking about. Who hasn't seen commercials or other forms of advertisements and direct marketing which tell you the product will be available at "this low price for a limited time only."

Very often the advertisement simply urges customers to buy at this discounted rate, but provides no date when it will go back to its regular price. Customers may not see an urgency to buy the product and in fact many of them may not purchase the product at all.

When the company gives a deadline regarding the length of time the product will be on sale, though, then it is prompting its customers to act by a certain date. It's almost a certainty that they'll see a surge in sales prior to the deadline. Now, you can understand why companies are so determined to use a deadline.

Time Constraints and Quality

Many individuals believe that deadlines adversely affect the quality of the end product. They believe if a project has to be completed in a short amount of time, then it cannot be given full justice. *But, reality shows quality is only compromised when the project is started at the last minute.*

Here's another example of the Parkinson's Law at work, only this time we are dealing with an insurance firm. An insurance agent has been given a goal of selling 50 policies in a month. However, he wastes the first twenty-five days of the deadline thinking, "There's still lots of time to sell these policies."

On the twenty-fifth day, though, he wakes up in a panic when it finally hits him that he only has five days left until deadline. He hasn't sold one policy and to sell fifty in five days would be difficult. It would even be more unlikely that he could do so without compromising quality.

If he had been more focused from day one of the deadline, then he would have only one or two policies left to sell. That would have been much easier and made more sense than what he's currently facing.

For every task you face during a day, you need to make a decision: "By what date must this job be completed?" If you have to, break the activity into smaller, more manageable goals. In this way, you can see how you are chopping the task down bit by bit.

A student, for example, decides on a particular date by which he needs to be finished studying a particular subject. He first examines the organization of the topic in order to discover the most logical way of breaking the subject matter down. He then assigns a goal for completion for every section, making sure he finishes by the deadline.

In a similar manner, a homemaker decides by what time the meal needs to be served and the cleaning up afterwards should be completed. She then breaks these steps accordingly.

You can do the same thing when you decide to read a book—especially if you have every intention of finishing it. Take the entire number of pages in the book and decide how many pages a day you need to read to be able to finish it by a particular date. You have just made reading a book a "time-bound" activity.

TWO

Even the terms we use in completing goals is indicative of how we feel about meeting them. We assign them to "deadlines," which implies the amount of pressure that exists to ensure they are completed. It certainly implies that this job is viewed as a burden. Not only that, but the closer you get to the final deadline, more is the pressure that you feel.

Consider, for a minute, how you would feel if you called them "life lines" or even "dates of fulfillment." Fulfillment, by the way, means the expression of happiness. You certainly do feel happiness as well as a sense of satisfaction when you successfully complete your job on time.

And if you used the term "fulfillment date" instead of deadline, you, no doubt, experience a "joy of completion."

Experiencing that "joy of completion" also has a hidden benefit. When you complete the work by the fulfillment date, you may have had to overcome many challenges in the process. Who hasn't had the sinking feeling of their laptop not working at a crucial time in a project or being faced with a new task in the middle of the one you're working on at the moment? Or the challenge could just be in the form of unexpected visitors.

In the pursuit of the joy of fulfillment, though, you face all of these challenges with a creative outlook and by using innovative methods. In this way, it really is possible to complete the project on time. Let's say, for example, that in the middle of your current assignment, you were handed a second one. This latter assignment is an emergency that has cropped up unexpectedly and can't wait until you have completed the current one. By completing both on time, you feel more confident. Not only that but you have increased your multitasking skills in the process as well. And that will come in handy in the future.

It may take a while for you to get into the habit of changing this term from "deadline" to "fulfillment date," but with a bit of practice, you'll get used to it. In fact, along with changing the name, you could also adjust your approach to these "fulfillment dates." Why not motivate yourself by rewarding yourself when you do reach this fulfillment date?

Promise yourself that if you complete the activity within a specified time period, you could take a holiday, buy a new outfit, or simply take a break to do one of your favorite things.

There may be times when the job is not completed and you are faced with what you consider failure. Do not be deterred but instead learn from the reasons the job was not accomplished. Gradually, you will develop the quality of completing jobs on time. This quality will also make you time-rich.

*Those who make the worst use of their time
are the first to complain of its brevity.*

– Jean de La Bruyère

TWO

Smart Tip to Manage your Time

SELECTION OF CLOTHES MADE EASY

"What do I wear today?" Does this problem take up too much of your time every day?

Women generally experience this issue daily. Those men who face this conundrum can also adopt the technique mentioned below.

To save time and find a solution to this problem, you could assign a color to each day, like red for Monday, blue for Tuesday, yellow for Wednesday, and so on. Similarly, set your closet according to the order of the days of the week. The clothes of one color could be placed together, so you can search in the color-specified pile for something to wear, according to the day.

Just imagine how much time you can save with this approach!

Section III

TIME AND TASK MANAGEMENT

TOOLS TO SAVE TIME

Ways to begin work

*Respect time.
Earn its trust with action.*

THREE

There is nothing more ironic than using one of the biggest "time-wasters" on beginning a project. When confronted with a new task or activity, the tendency of many people is to put it off. Many of us spend so much time to getting around to beginning it, that the time for actually doing that project may be gone.

You may think procrastination is an inevitable part of your workday as well as your personality, after all, you ask, isn't procrastination engineered into the human DNA?

It may seem so, but it doesn't have to be that way. Part of the problem is that we don't respect "time" like we do other things in our life. For example, if you went shopping and found exactly what you were looking for and it cost Rs 200, you would think twice before you bought something completely unrelated for Rs 200 just as a way of putting off buying your original item.

Most of us would grab the item we intended and buy it. We don't do that with time. Because of our apparent lack of respect for it, we don't treat it like the money in our wallet.

It doesn't have to be that way. We have already discussed some methods to make the best of our time. Below are some more suggestions on how to respect, and in the process, gain more time in your day to do what's necessary in a shorter amount of time than you're spending right now.

1. Begin work "before" the scheduled time

If your day begins like a typical person's day, it starts with procrastination even before you climb out of bed. It's called a "snooze" alarm. You delay the actual getting up and physically out of bed for as long as possible. Some individuals have such a hard time getting out of bed, they hit the snooze alarm three or even four times in the morning.

You do the math. When you hit the snooze alarm, let's say four times, and it's "only" a delay of "five more minutes," you have just used twenty minutes lying in bed. Doing what? Merely postponing the inevitable start of your day.

It feels good, sure, but what you probably didn't notice was that the effects of the groggy procrastination linger throughout the day, at the very least most of the morning.

Then when you sit down to work, you probably try to put it off as long as possible, which in effect is just another time-waster. You may do it even if the task is easy. So, you finally get it completed, but with this state of mind, chances are you have compromised its quality.

The solution? You should develop the habit of beginning your scheduled activities even before your normal start time. Though right now, you might be a bit skeptical about this or have excuses why you can't.

Let's start with the very beginning of your day again with that pesky alarm clock. What would happen if when the alarm rings the first time, you resisted hitting that snooze button and instead got out of bed?

In actuality, that earlier start to your day will make you feel better. Not only that, but you'll also find that your actions have been rewarded by alleviating unnecessary stress.

For example, let's say you reach the office a little bit earlier than your normal start time. Your body is created in a way that from a physiological perspective it's in perfect harmony between 8 a.m. and 9 a.m. So, if you arrive even one hour earlier, you can save yourself from staying past your quitting time by some two hours after 6 p.m. to complete your work. That means you'll be efficiently finishing your work on time.

2. Dedicate time for important tasks

For vital tasks, choose a time when no one will be around. Select a portion of the day when you know will be the most quiet and you are less likely to be interrupted or delayed in any way.

Let's say you have an activity that requires total concentration to complete. Your choices are either doing it late at night or early in the morning. This is when most people are asleep and your chances of getting disturbed are low. It's also great to choose one of these two time periods, because it's more difficult to go out and get a cup of tea or get involved in a good television program. Since you are well aware of this, the temptation doesn't arise. What does happen is the completion of 1-2 hours of vital tasks.

If you're saying that you already are an early riser, then how could you possibly get up any earlier? Before you build up a mountain of excuses, let's start looking at this situation a bit differently. Ask yourself, where and when you could make time to do this. Ponder on this and then be alert for an answer to come to you. You could take this time out during a weekend or holiday. Or you could wait after hours at the office. Once you are sure that everyone around you has left, then you can start the project.

The following example is a perfect illustration of this concept.

> Although committed to his search for the supreme truth, a seeker couldn't find the time to meditate on a regular basis. After giving it careful thought, he believed his only option was to wake up at 4 a.m., meditate, and then go back to sleep. Then he would wake up at his usual time. He succeeded in making this a habit because his body was trained to achieve goals like these once he resolved without any doubts that this was what he wanted.

Once you make a committed decision in your life that you're going to do something, then even if you meet certain challenges, you'll achieve it. The opposite though is also true. If the full intent of your mind is not behind your decision or your desire, you will always find excuses why you couldn't achieve that goal, desire, or habit. The decision to meditate early in the morning was chosen with care. There was no one around at that hour to stop him or disturb him, which meant he effectively eliminated his excuses.

The seeker of truth, though, noticed other benefits as well from his sincere and burning desire. He achieved a state where he was able to meditate for many hours without any difficulty or interruption. Thus, when you resolve—and truly intend—to achieve a goal, you will automatically "make" the time to get it completed.

3. Organize similar activities together

It's true that every task you are facing on any given day requires its own approach in order for you to complete it properly. But if you group similar tasks together, then you have created a smooth flow in completing them, so that there is no sense of interruption when you go from one task to the next.

Let's say, in the course of a day, you need to prepare for two separate presentations, write three articles, send four emails, and provide and disperse information. If you group them according to the type of task, you will find yourself in the flow of work—going with the current as it were and not against it. Once you have done this, then place a time limit on these activities. Now, you are not only in the flow of your workday, but you are "forcing" yourself to concentrate by giving yourself a deadline. Otherwise, you would idle your time away, procrastinating over one or more of the groupings.

This idea works just as efficiently out of the office as in it. Suppose, you need to buy several items. Instead of making a separate trip to do this, you could couple it with either your morning or evening commute to work. Or, you may decide to shop when you take your children to school or pick them up after school.

You can do the same thing when you are shopping. You probably have already noticed that in the mall, similar objects are displayed together in one section. If your goal is to buy something specific and leave without wasting time, you will head straight to its area.

Take a good look at how your home is organized. The coffee pot is usually beside the kitchen sink with coffee cups stored above it. All of your stationery items are stored in the same place, most likely in a desk drawer where you do your writing.

This organization is, of course, extended to your work office. All documents can be found in one area, usually in a file cabinet of some type and sorted by topic. You wouldn't expect to find health insurance papers stuck in a recipe book.

4. Keep items in pairs

Yes, there really is a reason for this. How often have you been at home and something that needs to be done at work pops into your mind? It works the other way as well. You are working at the office and you remember something that has to get done at home. This seems to happen all the time.

It may be something as simple as nail clippers. You need to clip your nails, but you couldn't do it at home, but, you remember it at work. And you don't have a clipper available.

Start making a list of such items that you need to purchase so you can have one at home and the other at work. In this way, you'll have one of them at your fingertips whether you're at home or in your office. In the long-term, this will save you more time than you could imagine. Below is a list of a few of the items you can buy in pairs. You can add your own to this list.

- Different colors of pens

- Diary
- Nail clipper
- Spectacles
- Dictionary
- Envelopes
- Charger
- Stationery
- Reading books
- Shoe polish

After thinking about it some, you will discover that you'll be making changes to this list as well as routinely begin to buy in pairs out of habit. Some individuals, of course, will feel that this will increase their expenses. But those who understand the importance and value of time, will value this practice.

Then there are those times when you take an item from one place with every intent of returning it to its rightful place. But then you simply forget or leave it in another, fully intending to remember where you have laid it down.

If you have to expend time searching over your house for a required item, that is, indeed, a waste of time. There's a simple solution to this. Simply tie the pen, the stapler, and other items with a string so that they can't be taken far from where they are normally stored. Yes, that means you will have to go to those items when you want to use them. But, you will always know where they are.

5. Create a reminder system

What's the first thing you do when you get home?

You may place the keys in a drawer, then you go into the kitchen and open the refrigerator door, or it could be something like taking off your shoes.

In essence, the larger question you're answering is, what is the first thing you look at? It's here you can place a note you are sure to see that will remind you of tasks you need to do.

If it's a drawer, that would be a perfect location for reminders. Let's say that you do keep your keys in a drawer when you get home. You can place a chit, or a reminder, in the first drawer you open. But the catch is that you always need to put the note in the same drawer daily. Let's say you need to call someone when you get home. Then before you leave for work that day, place your toddler's toy phone in there. That's the perfect reminder that you need to make a call.

If you decide to follow this method, then you have to develop the habit of opening this drawer every day. This will ensure that you get the reminders, which will save you from forgetting things or tasks.

6. Perform multi-switching

Many individuals have the wrong idea about what the term "multitasking" means. They assume that because they are working on multiple tasks throughout the day, they are "multitasking." In this case, this term is a misnomer. In truth, what you are really doing is "multi-switching." Think about it for a moment and you will see this is a more accurate description.

Nobody can really perform more than one activity at a time, which means nobody can do multi-tasking. You can't watch television while you read a book. You read the book, then look up at the television to see what's playing on it, and then go back to reading the book. This is multi-switching.

Suppose, you have to work on multiple projects. You can divide all those projects into small bits, and work on those bits every day.

Multi-switching means immediately shifting to another bit after completing one bit. This is what saves you time, not multi-tasking.

There are individuals who perform only one task during the day. It's not until after that task has been completed that they consider what they should take up next. This, though, can take a lot of time to complete the activities. With the aid of multi-switching throughout the day, you can progress on many tasks in a day.

The only caveat with multi-switching is this: once you lay an activity aside to work on another, you need to remember where you had left off. In this way, when you return, you are not wasting valuable time wondering where to start again. After you put down every activity, you need to make a note of how much of the job has been completed.

Let's say, for example, that you're reading two books. Not only that, but you want to finish them as quickly as possible. This is the perfect time to practice multi-switching. You simply read a few pages from both of the books daily, and before you know it, you will have completed both books. But, you wouldn't do this, though, without leaving a bookmark in the books so you know where you left off. The alternative is to waste time trying to figure out where to pick up the storyline.

In much the same way, you must be diligent about maintaining progress on your daily tasks. While you are multi-switching from one activity to another, keep track of where you left off, so you can turn right back to that area when you are ready to return to it. This not only saves much time but also enables you to do several activities in a day.

7. Work with a stopwatch

Yes, you read that correctly. If you haven't had a chance to familiarize yourself with a stopwatch, this is the perfect time to do so. You're about to learn how you can use one in order to more thoroughly inspect your time schedule. What you are about to do is create a "time diary."

You're about to ask yourself the question where you can save time and the stopwatch is going to help you answer that question. Upon waking up in the morning, set the stopwatch for each task you have planned. As you start a new activity, switch on the stop watch. You're going to record how much time it took to complete each task.

Once you have an estimate on the length of the activity, your next question will be: "Where can I save time?" You're going to record these figures in your time diary, which you'll be updating continuously using the times you've noted with the stopwatch.

Here's an example. As you prepare for work, set the stopwatch in order to see how long this process takes. If you can see that you take an hour for this, then write this in your time diary. Now, review what's involved in getting ready for work and ask yourself if you could shave fifteen minutes off this series of activities. If you believe you can, then work toward that. And when you do, you'll have an extra fifteen minutes to your day.

At first, this might not seem like a lot of time. These fifteen minutes you save on a daily basis, you might want to invest them in the art projects you've been dreaming about. Think about it. Fifteen minutes saved daily and accumulated over a period of a year can set your life in a new and exciting direction and help you achieve success and gain happiness.

Below you'll find illustrated examples of a typical stopwatch timetable. If you want, feel free to use these examples as a template for your time diary.

STOP-WATCH TIME-TABLE		
Activity	Time it took	Time it should take
Getting ready for office	1 hour	45 min
Breakfast		
Lunch		
Book reading		
Time on phone throughout the day		
Time spent building castles in the air		
Commute		
Exercise		
Cleaning		
Searching for things		

FREEDOM FROM THE MENTAL BURDEN OF WORK

Change your current modus operandi

> *By not giving importance to your time,
> you reduce your own importance.*

Are your daily activities planned ahead of time? There's an easy way to find out. Ask yourself the questions outlined below.

- Do you feel that whatever you do is unplanned, unsystematic, and unproductive?
- Do you end up doing everything at the last moment due to a lot of interruptions?
- Are you constantly struggling to finish some task or the other?
- Do you feel stressed or nervous due to the changing priorities of tasks?
- Do you make daily lists for tasks but are unable to follow them?

If you answered yes to most of these questions, then your daily activities aren't planned very well, if at all. What's more, you could certainly learn something from a few simple but effective time-management strategies.

In a normal daily routine, you naturally come up with interesting thoughts and ideas, as well as you are being given important papers or telephone numbers. Unfortunately, you're in such a hurry that you take them and then stash these items somewhere. You don't mean to, but usually you forget about them, sometimes even forgetting where you tucked them away. The bottom line is that you seldom go back over these pieces of information later like you promised you would.

Don't blame your memory when this occurs. That's not where the problem lies. The issue is more of a physical organizational problem. You don't have at hand a reliable method that facilitates the gathering and managing of these important papers, emails, notes, and other information. When you don't have a proper storage facility or even a temporary holding place for this type of information, then you are bound to forget them—at least part of the time. The truth of the matter is that you're still on the lowest rung of time management skills.

That may be the bad news, but the good news is that with a few changes, you'll be on your way to the upper rungs of time management.

So where do you start? How about with yourself?

Below are some tips and techniques to help you step up to manage your time better.

Don't be a slave to mood, memory, and environmnet

Waiting for the right mood and environment is something that all the lethargic people of our country are doing. If only someone would be able to give them the right mood and the perfect environment or atmosphere. But that's impossible.

The majority of people who procrastinate on starting a new activity say they are waiting for the right mood or inspiration to strike them. If you're one of them, then you are in for a long wait. It is only by taking action that feelings or desire to carry out the activities is born.

There's only one way you're going to achieve your goals, let alone get through the day achieving the maximum amount of work possible. That's by regulating your feelings and emotions. You may be looking at the problem backwards. You're waiting to be inspired in order to work.

You can wait forever if that's your mindset. What you need is to get to work and then be inspired. Sounds impossible? Not at all.

You need to get your feelings and emotions under control, regularize them, and then you will be able to tackle your tasks head on, regardless of how you feel about these activities. But rest assured it won't take long, once you start working on a project, the inclination to work on it will follow.

The truth of the matter is when all is said and done, your action is directly within your control, even if your feelings and desires are not. You can't wait for feelings towards the project or your interest in it to grow but you can, nevertheless, begin the project with your actions.

If you follow this principle, then regardless of the activity you have facing you, there's only one way to begin. You start with the knowledge that interest will automatically come. You will also soon realize that to achieve it, you need to be completely focused.

Once you learn that even if the mood doesn't strike you or the atmosphere isn't perfect, then simply work faster on the project. What? The task which isn't drawing you in, perform that activity quickly. If it's a presentation you must write, then write faster. If you're not inspired to call a client, then take a deep breath and call as quickly as you can.

You would be surprised what happens when you try not only to start it quickly but to finish the activity as soon as possible. The speed with which you execute the task prevents your mind from becoming a slave to your moods. Once you become a slave to moods, you will discover that you're unsuccessful.

What would happen if your wife, mother, or sister waited for the proper mood to strike her before she made supper? How many days a week would you estimate you'd eat at home? Now you see just how important it is to get rid of the idea that "I'm going to write this presentation when the mood strikes me and only when I'm in the mood to do it."

Instead, say to yourself that I'm going to start writing this presentation and my mood will change to meet this new image of me. If that's possible—and we know it is—then this is exactly what you need to do in order to free yourself from the moods holding you back. And before you realize it, you'll be completing your work on time. And then before long perhaps even ahead of your deadlines.

Many individuals have the bad habit of relying on their memory instead of writing the activities they must work on down on paper or input them into their electronic calendar. They pile and store tasks that need to be done into their memory one by one. You can see in your eye's mind what an unstable, tottering pile of information is towering in their mind.

Imagine, for a moment, that you've been asked to complete a specific job. You don't have a day planner with you and you don't have a notebook either that you can jot this down in. So, you commit this to memory—or so you think. Now, you've added this to the "work pile" in your mind and made it just a bit bigger. This increases your mental burden.

Not only that, but this task is very much hanging in mid-air in the middle of your mind. You have no definite plan on how you're going to accomplish it. You have no time limit set for its completion.

Let's say your supervisor has requested that you send him that important report. Now, with no way to make a note of it, you find yourself (through no fault of your own) a slave to your memory. It should come as no surprise when you completely forget about this "imaginary" project and you don't send it.

To be honest, without any written to-do list, this is the procedure you find yourself following on most days and in most cases. You now understand why you can't recall even one or two of the activities you must do, let alone complete them. And now you can see why it's far better for you to create your own personal system that will free you from the slavery to your memory.

Many individuals discover that as hostages to their moods, memory, and the atmosphere, they end up completing the first activity that comes to mind, even though it may not be the most important one. After all, they don't have any type of to-do list created. They take on this random activity first thing in the morning and then work the entire day in an effort to finish it. What's more, if you've ever done this, the odds are you'll complete those activities which you enjoy doing. This isn't necessarily a bad thing; as long as you're working on the important activities as well. But if you are not, then it's going to lead to a lot of stress.

By operating in this manner, you fail to control your work environment, and so it starts controlling you. Now the sad part is that more than likely, you begin to face more and more jobs in which you're pressured to complete some of the most important ones hastily, instead of giving them the time they truly deserve.

In the 21st century, you have more ideas and tasks clouding your mind than ever before. You have a string of daily emails that pop up as well as other electronic messages. Then you have a mindful of "imaginary" tasks that seem to be increasing all the time demanding your attention. If you allow in all the events swirling around you, they could be overloading your mind. It's no wonder you feel as if you've become a slave to mood, memory, and atmosphere.

If you find this happening to you, don't feel bad and don't even think for a moment you are lazy. That's far from the truth. You've just found yourself in a rut of postponing your own progress, you might say.

It's time we look at three new levels of time management and understand how you can break free from this bondage. This system is called the "Result Producing System." It has been developed especially by focusing on the unprecedented needs of this era and with several vital factors in mind: reducing struggle, reducing stress, and reducing the time you're using.

Smart Tip to Manage your Time

FIND TIME TO WALK

How can I find the recommended one to one-and-a-half hours for taking a walk?

First, you should realize you don't need to walk one to one-and-a-half hours in one chunk of time. You can break up your walking time into 20-minute periods. Then, whenever you get an available 20 minutes, you can take a walk.

Even 20 minutes on some days may seem like a long time to be away from your work. If that's the case, then while going for work, leave your home earlier and park your car 20 minutes away from the building, and walk the rest of the way. In this way, you are sure to get at least two 20 minute walks—coming in to work and going home.

If you take the bus or a train to your workplace, then if suitable, get off one stop before your workplace and walk the rest of the way. This can be repeated on the way back home too. When you do this, you don't feel as if you're taking time away from your daily schedule.

RESULT PRODUCING SYSTEM

Three Levels of Time Management

Draw up a rough plan for the next day before going to bed every night.
With this, the hardest tasks are easily accomplished in the morning.

Are you working with a smoke of chaos trailing behind you, choking your productivity? Are you just getting the job done in minutes under the deadline accompanied with a big sigh of relief. "Another fire put out," you say. But, wait! What do you see over there, another ember burning? Another task teetering on the cliff of being late? Where did that come from?

You know how tiring that can be. You know, first hand, that sinking feeling in your stomach of being totally overwhelmed by the volume of work that seemingly appeared out of nowhere and has you constantly shuffling your priorities—again.

Most of the times though, the problem isn't the extent of the work as much as it is the system you use for collecting these directives, filing them, and then prioritizing them. What? You say you don't really have a system, except your memory? While your memory is a good start, it isn't a flawless method of collection. When you have no system or a broken system like too many to-do lists, your time management is at, what many individuals label as, Level 0.

At this stage of management, your tasks are just floating in the air or even up in smoke.

Here's what we mean by this. A task comes to your attention. You take it and tuck it away in that cloud of smoke behind your head we've been talking about. "I'm not going to forget about it," you say. "It's far too important. It's obviously something I'm going to remember."

Then your manager emails you asking you to send him a project report. When you open that email, you're in the middle of putting out some other task-related fire. So, you read the email and think to yourself, "I'll send that to him as soon as I'm done here."

Then you turn your attention to the fire. . . umm. . . task at hand. Another request up in smoke. You can see how anyone even with the best of intentions can forget an item here or there.

That's just one day. You wake up the following morning, and look at your planner (if you have one) and you don't see any fires burning. You see no assignments due for today or pressing for tomorrow.

Then you think back to the day before, pulling a task from the cloud of smoke that followed you to work. By the way, because it is smoke, you can't see too far into that cloud. This means you don't really know what's in the recesses of the cloud that should also be accomplished.

Mastering the Art of Time Management | 67

Thus, at Level 0, you're seemingly planning your day from smoke. It's very likely that you're doing what you are interested in and not necessarily what needs to be done for the day.

You're not in control of your working environment so much as your environment is in charge of you. You're constantly discovering still another project labeled urgent and on fire.

If you're struggling at Level 0 on the time-management system, then you have no systematic way of organizing and prioritizing your projects. You probably don't even have a lone piece of paper on which you scribble your assignments. Undoubtedly, your emails, memos, files, and notes are without exception in a disarray. As a result, you feel overwhelmed, disorganized, and totally out of control.

This does not mean you are a shirker or slacker if you are at Level 0. Far from it. You are in all probability working harder than your colleagues—with less to show for it. Except for the amount of stress you're under, of course.

It only signifies that you have no system of prioritizing and managing your work load. This is a hindrance to your productivity because you're only working on assignments which are urgent. Or you reach into the cloud of smoke over your head, like it was a magician's hat, and pull out a long-forgotten task—which immediately takes priority over everything you're doing at the moment, because it's been back in the smoke so long that it's now urgent and nearly on fire itself.

Now you can understand why you seem to work longer hours than your colleagues, because you probably do. You may be a workaholic and yet still be at Level 0 in your time management style. This lack of organization, in fact, may be the reason you *are* a workaholic. Not only that, but the lack of a system also leads to a habit of postponing the development of projects.

Let's examine how you can improve your performance by learning how the other three levels of a new time management system, called the Result Producing System, works. It's ideally suited to the way you work in this modern era.

Urgency and importance dominated the old school time management models. This thinking is fading and being replaced with a system that involves "less" of everything: less effort, less stress, and less of everything that's unnecessary.

In the **Result Producing System**, you'll move from Level 0 and choose to work at one of the other three:

Level 1: Tasks in writing

Level 2: Tasks in order

Level 3: Goals in control

LEVEL 1: TASKS IN WRITING

Level 1 can change your entire outlook on your job and your relationship to the tasks you've been charged with. This level may seem like a small, incremental move, but attached to it is a large benefit.

Typically, the average person doesn't write his tasks anywhere. When, on the off chance that he does, it's not at all unusual to see it in the form of notes posted on the refrigerator, on napkins from various restaurants, hotel stationery, and a journal. He may have keyed in his assignments in a computer file called "Pending" and then another called "Latest Pending."

The result? It's no different than being at Level 0. Tasks are captured nearly everywhere, which becomes the equivalent to being captured nowhere.

What does it take to be at Level 1?

To go from Level 0 to Level 1, you only have to make one change. You have to get all of your projects down in writing in the same place. Use only one "dedicated writing tool."

It doesn't matter what it is. It could be a small pocket diary or notebook. It could be a piece of software on your computer or even an app on your mobile phone. Whatever location you choose, remain committed and consistent in using it.

If you choose a small diary or a notebook, you must remember to take it everywhere with you. That's why an app on your mobile looks so attractive right about now. Using your computer may become a bit problematic, just because you're not always going to be dragging it along with you. Besides that, it's a little inconvenient to open just to write in one small task. You procrastinate and say to yourself, "I'll put this in the computer file when I get home." Before you can say "fire," you've got a cloud of smoke following you around again.

Write it down—in one place

Your sole responsibility right now is to merely ensure that all tasks can be found in one place and you can see all of them at the same time. You're not even required to categorize them.

Your new mantra is: "Write it down—in one place." You'll repeat it until this mantra becomes a part of you—a routine way of doing business.

You'll also acquire the habit of carrying your "dedicated writing tool" with you wherever you go. Take it not only to work but to social engagements as well. Such as any civic meeting, meeting at your children's school, to the movies, and yes, if suitable, even into the bathroom when you're taking a shower. If you get some ideas in the shower, you can put them down in your dedicated writing tool. If your boss calls and gives you a task, write it in this tool. If you make a commitment to a friend, again note it at the same place.

Every time you are about to begin your work, you will refer to this tool and this list, and then start working accordingly.

Taking one step at a time

It's best to develop your organizational skills one step at a time, and instill habits slowly and methodically. This will ensure that you make this part of your normal workday and not something you only do occasionally when you think of it.

Your new habit can now be stated easily: Get it out of your head and onto paper or your mobile. Think of it. You're in a meeting and an action item is mentioned that will need your attention later. You note it down. Even if you forget about it before the end of the meeting, you've got the item in writing. And then you'll always look at that list the next time you start working and—voila!—you're reminded of it. The same thing occurs when you're at a social gathering. Someone provides you with their phone number or email address, simply note it down right there.

Even this small step will boost your productivity significantly. It will reduce your stress and save your time. This occurs because you stop forgetting items, you no longer are losing vital information, and most importantly, you'll always know where to find the next action item that deserves your attention before it turns into a burning ember.

Level 1 Paperwork Management

When you're working at Level 1 paperwork management, all that's involved is that you file all of your paperwork (yes, all of it) into one large tray at your home office or at work. As you gather more and the papers mount, here again, you may want to store specific ones at the office and others at home.

When you do this, you've created a "dedicated filing tool." You'll no longer have loose papers floating about. You won't again stuff some paper in a desk drawer, some post-it note anywhere else on your desk, or incoming letters anyplace else. Your "dedicated filing tool" has now become your one and only place to collect your information. You can discard those items when you're done with them. This is your new filing system. It may appear to be too simple but you'll see that it will make a world of difference.

What about emails?

You can keep all the emails associated with the tasks embedded in your "dedicated writing tool" in a separate file in your email system called "Committed Tasks." Create a file with this label and move all relevant task-related emails from your inbox into this folder.

This is where they stay. You work with these emails out of this folder. Only when the task is completed can you move it to another location. You may decide to archive the original emails or simply delete them. The bottom line, though, at Level 1, is that you work from one file and one file only.

It's best to have one email account. This prevents multiple inboxes that can only too easily lead to confusion. If it's simply impossible to have only one email account, then apply this same principle to all of your accounts.

However, at Level 1, it's fine if you start out with just having one dedicated writing tool without the filing or email management at the beginning. The important point is that if you're currently working at Level 0, you get a simple start.

LEVEL 2 TIME MANAGEMENT

Tasks in Order

After you've practiced the Level 1 time management tenets for several months, and if you are now habituated and comfortable using that level, you're ready to move on to Level 2.

At Level 2, you create the habit of prioritizing what's on your schedule. You'll need to learn how to divide your work into two sections: Need to do (Needs) and Wish/Want to do (Aspirations).

This starts by the creation of these two sections in your "dedicated writing tool." These sections are self-explanatory. Assignments and tasks that are required by your present employer or your business or any important task for your home gets listed under the "Need to Do" section. Any assignment not considered critical or is something you'd like to do when the moment is right will go under the "Wish List."

How to decide placement

How can you know under which heading your assignments belong? Obviously, much of the decision will be mostly a judgment call on your part. You just need to be consistent in your placement. It'll make it easier and quicker if you maintain consistency filing similar tasks together if possible. If you do this, the repetition will have this nearly reduced to a habit.

Here are some examples below so you can get an idea of what we mean.

You've given your word and committed yourself to accomplishing a task for someone. That goes under the Need List. By contrast, you'd love to take some time and go to a movie. Unless your job is that of a movie critic, this goes into your Wish List.

While you're working one day, you suddenly get an idea you believe will improve conditions at work. This, though, is not an important project or something that is expected of you. You place it under your Wish List. When you place an item on your Wish List, that doesn't mean it has to stay there forever. At some point, the circumstances may change and it will become a need and not just a wish.

Your Wish List will undoubtedly contain a list of items you can't do right now as well as items you don't want to complete at the moment. Another way to look at your Wish List is to put tasks there that you either can't or won't work on this week or perhaps even this month. You can decide the period, although the recommended period is one week.

When you make a Need and Wish List, you're freeing yourself mentally. It's human nature to believe that one day you'll suddenly perform all the tasks on both of these lists magically. Don't hold your breath. The likelihood of this is slim to none. So, don't worry about having placed many things on your Wish List that may never get done. The completion of the tasks on your Need List is far more important.

If you haven't used a computer to build your to-do list yet, this would be a fine time to switch, but it certainly isn't mandatory. An alternative to placing both lists on your computer would be to transfer only your Need List there. Your Wish List can remain on your dedicated writing tool.

Along a similar vein, you can retain two apps in your mobile or two sections within a single app. However you decide to do this, the idea behind these actions is simple: create two lists and focus on the Need List first.

Every week or every month, read your Wish List to see if you want to move any item to the Need List. This weekly or monthly review is at the core of Level 2 time management.

The mantra at Level 2 for task management is: "Write it Down and Split it Up." This one move will improve your productivity. But, to be even more productive, before you begin your work, ponder for a few moments if there is anything you have to add to your Need List. After that, decide on the top three "Most Important Tasks" or MITs from this list.

Then ensure to complete these three items. If you do them early in your workday, you have the satisfaction of knowing they're not hanging over your head anymore. What's more, you've now freed up your time to accomplish other items from the list.

You probably already realize that not everything on your Need List will get accomplished. There always will be an item or two or more that you won't be able to finish. That's to be expected. Remember that this list is an ever-changing flowing list. As you complete one or two actions, you'll find yourself adding one or two other tasks, maybe more. If you should ever find yourself in the position in which your Need List contains no actionable items, then, by all means move on and pluck items from your Wish List.

Information Management or Paperwork

To manage your paperwork, you will create a "Need Tray/File" and a "Wish Box."

Any paperwork that is important and is associated with any item on your Need List goes into the Need Tray or Need File. Remember that a Need Task indicates that it must get accomplished within a day, a week, or a month, as per your decision. You'll place everything else into a large Wish Box or Wish File. If you'd like, you can create further files or place stickers and categorize your Wish Box or File. At the very least, have the two major files in place. Everything you receive in regards to all your tasks goes into one of these two locations. Once the task is completed, then you can discard the paperwork.

Emails

When you're working with email management at level 2, you'll create two folders. The first is called "Need List" and the second "Wish List." These, as you may have already figured, should be kept in a location other than your email inbox.

Every piece of email that relates to your Need List obviously will be filed in the Need List folder. Everything else can be filed in your Wish List folder. At Level 2, you can get the satisfaction of emptying your inbox. All of your mail can go into one of these folders or labels. If you'd like, you can create "sub-folders" under these two main priority lists, depending on the categories. You may also set up rules that automatically move the emails to these folders. For example, you received a newsletter that can be read at any time. It can be automatically moved to your Wish List folder or to a sub-folder you labeled "Newsletters."

As you work on your emails, you'll want to make it a priority to finish moving them to each of these lists. Only then, transfer your focus to the Need List. Thereafter, you may want to decide if you want to delete, archive, or move them into different folders once the items are completed.

Thus, level 2 will make things a lot easier to manage and enhance your productivity. But it's level 3 that will take you toward your goals. We shall learn about it in the next chapter.

The great dividing line between success and failure can be expressed in five words: "I did not have time."

– Franklin Field

Goal Management System

Level 3 Time Management

*"I am complete,
and from completeness all tasks are completed in perfect time."
Repeat this phrase constantly and become complete.*

Are you ready to transform your time management system into a goal management system? Are you ready to take the reins of your career and your life, and go from merely working day-to-day to working to ensure your plans for the future actually manifest into reality?

Up until this moment, you've dealt with Need and Wish Lists—everything you need in order to handle all of your tasks, assignments, work commitments, and promises to others and yourself in a timely fashion.

Now that you've got Levels 1 and 2 under your belt, it's time to move on to Level 3, which in some ways is the most exciting. It's at this level you'll begin to factor your goals into your daily schedule.

This is where the time management system transforms itself into a goal management system.

Instead of keeping one Need List and one Wish List, you'll begin creating multiple goals lists along with one Wish list. It may sound a bit complicated upon first hearing about it, but moving up from Level 2 to Level 3 is easier than you think.

The chart on the following page will give you an idea of how you can use Level 3 to your advantage.

There are 4 steps to achieve Level 3:

Step 1: Annual Goals

The first thing Level 3 asks of you is to write down your annual goals. From now on, you can plan on doing this once a year. If you've never thought realistically about where you want to be a year from now, it's time to give it some thought.

You'll write down no more than 7 goals because this is the maximum your brain can handle effectively. When you do this, you'll want to try to divide them into various areas of your life. For example, you may want to label the areas as physical, mental, social, financial, and spiritual.

If you feel more comfortable, you can write down your goals for the next six months or nine months instead. Then at the beginning of next year, you can create annual ones. If you want, you can write your yearly goals from one birthday to another.

At this point, don't worry about how specific or vague these goals are. They can be specific goals like point 1 below or generic goals like point 6.

Below is a sample of what your goals list may resemble.

Goal	Type of Goal
1. Attain ideal weight of 70 Kg	Physical
2. Spend quality time with my child	Social
3. Increase savings and investments by 40%	Financial
4. Start a new part-time business	Financial
5. Read 10 books this year	Mental
6. Improve my practice of meditation	Spiritual
7. Spend time serving my community	Social /Spiritual

Step 2: MITs

What's an MIT? It is the Most Important Task in your day.

At Level 3, you decide that every morning before you begin working, you'll write your MITs for each goal area you created. Then write down the tasks that must get accomplished that do not have any goal under the heading of "Other Needs."

Below is an example of what this will look like when you're done. You'll notice that some of these goals have more than one MIT, while others have none assigned to them. That's fine. In fact, each day when you allocate these tasks, you'll discover that you may be assigning vastly different tasks to your goals daily.

All of your other tasks will be assigned to your "Need List" under the category "Others" along with two or three key work-related goals.

Goal	MITs
1. Attain ideal weight of 70 Kg	Exercise for 45 minutes today.
2. Spend quality time with my child	Pick my kid from school and spend at least 15 minutes of quality time with him/her.
3. Increase savings and investments by 40%	—
4. Grow company sales by 30%	- Speak to a friend to collect information on new client. - Attend Weekly Pipeline Review.
5. Read 10 books this year	Read 15 pages of book *The Source* today
6. Improve my practice of meditation	Meditate for 15 minutes today.
7. Spend time serving my community	—
8. Others	- File income tax return. - Get Mom birthday card for tomorrow. - Attend Accounts Meeting in company and prepare a report.

In the above example, there is one key work-related goal where an employee's goal is to increase sales by 30%. Only tasks relevant to key work-related goals will be mentioned as MITs under that. All other tasks in the company unrelated to that goal will go under "Others."

An easy way to maintain an MIT List using 7 goals and an 8th "Others" list can be done by taking an A4 size paper—that's a standard 8½ x 11 inch—and folding it in, so that eight folds are created. Thus, any A4 paper becomes your planning tool. Here is how an A4 page folded into 8 parts will look like.

Goal 1	Goal 2
Goal 3	Goal 4
Goal 5	Goal 6
Goal 7	Others

You can fill in the names of the 7 goals you have in this sheet and under each box you can list MITs for that day. All other tasks that "need" to be done will go under "Others."

Instead of paper, the above listing can be done on a computer or on a mobile phone app. The key to Level 3 is that your MITs should be clearly seen. Hence, writing on a paper and putting up on your desk is the most effective way to focus on your MITs. If you don't want people to know your goals, you can always use short forms.

Step 3: Wish List

Like in Level 2, you can also maintain a Wish List where tasks that are not an MIT or don't belong on the Need List (under "Others") can be maintained. This can be done in a notebook or in a separate section on your computer or mobile.

Step 4: Complete MITs first

Now, here's the most important part: get the MITs done first, if possible all of them. First thing in the morning, before you even check your email, get that first MIT done. Clear away all distractions, and be sure to focus on only that task until it's done. When you're done, reward yourself. But be sure to move on to your next MIT shortly after that.

When you're working on your MITs, set a timer if you like, or otherwise just focus on that task for as long as possible. Don't let yourself get distracted from them. If you should get interrupted, write down any request or incoming tasks into your Needs (in "Other") or Wish List, and get back to working on your MIT.

At this point, you may be tempted to multi-task, but don't. At first, you may find it difficult to fight back that "multi-tasking" habit. But when you're tempted to do something else "just-for-a-minute," stop yourself. Take a moment and then breathe deeply. Refocus your mind. You're now ready to turn back to the task at hand.

Here you have it. Four simple yet powerful steps to lift you from

Level 2 where all you were doing was managing your time, to Level 3 where you are finally working toward your goals.

At the start of every day, look at your MITs. Was there something you didn't get to complete yesterday? Update your MIT listing accordingly. Do the same thing with your Wish List. Check if there is any item that needs to be moved to the Need list under the "Others" section if you have time for it on that day.

What about Paperwork Management?

You'll create one file in which all goals-related paperwork will go. You'll also make an "Other Needs" file or tray and a Wish Box for all of your other filing.

If you think it would be better for your personal style, you can have a file for each of your goals. That, however, may be a bit ambitious. You might want to try having just one file and then expand that if you feel the need.

What about emails?

At Level 3 management, you'll do exactly what you did in the previous level. But here, you'll also add a Goals folder or label. This requires you to move all of your MIT-related emails for specific goals here. If you'd like, you can also create a sub-folder or label for each goal.

You also have a new mantra to recite at this level of management:

"Aim it straight. Think it up (MITs). Write it down. Get it done."

	How is work managed	Key Tools	How to organize papers and files	How to organize emails
Level 1: Tasks in writing	Everything captured (in writing)	One collection tool	One capture tray	One Dedicated Tasks Folder or Label
Level 2: Tasks in order	Everything prioritized	Two Lists: Need List and Wish List	One "Needs" Tray or File and one Wish Box	One Needs Folder or Label, one Wish Folder or Label. Other sub folders or labels
Level 3: Goals in control	Most Important Things first	Two Lists: 1) Goals List that includes Need List in "Others" Section and 2) Wish List	One Goals file (or multiple files), one Need File or Tray, and one Wish Box	One Goals Folder or Label with sub folders or labels, one Needs Folder or Label, one Wish Folder or Label. Other sub folders or labels.

Summary of the Result Producing System

Here are the three levels we have discussed so far.

Level 1: Tasks in writing

Level 2: Tasks in order

Level 3: Goals in control

You've familiarized yourself with the three levels of organization we've talked about so far. Decide what level you feel most comfortable working at. This means you choose the level you feel you can master with relative ease.

It doesn't matter which level you choose. What matters more is that you're confident you can continue working at this level competently. If you feel you're not quite ready to jump to Level 3, then don't. Stay with Level 2 if it's working for you right now. You can always review these processes every couple of months to determine if you're ready to go to the next level.

As you're working with this system, keep in mind that along with time management, you'll also have to master organizing the paperwork or file management along with accompanying emails.

The table on the preceding page summarizes all of these points.

The crucial aspect of successfully implementing the Result Producing System is discipline. If discipline seems like a harsh word to you, then think of it as forming habits. And in this system, you'll be forming habits incrementally—one level at a time.

You've probably already tried implementing any number of organizational management strategies in your work, household duties, and in your attempts to launch a new business. What has happened? If you're like many of us, you get excited at the prospect of finally getting a grip on your work and goals. And you work with a certain amount of zeal and enthusiasm you haven't felt in a long time.

And then...

What happens? It feels as if you miss one day in your habits and suddenly all work toward your previous organization has disappeared and you're left with... well paperwork scattered all over in a variety of locations (some of which you swear you didn't put it there).

Then you make a vow to try again. And you're doing fine and then... BOOM. That's the sound of you dropping those habits. If you're like most people, you get discouraged and just quit trying.

Habits are hard to change. Bad habits are hard to get rid of and good habits can be just as difficult to adopt successfully. But that doesn't mean you should just quit.

If you intend on cultivating good habits and shedding the bad ones, then you should be aware even before you start that this is no small challenge. But it's a challenge that will be worth it. Be prepared to put much energy and effort toward these changes as well as focus. Also, before you begin to change any habit, you must be sure that you are motivated.

Because of all these reasons, you should not try to change too many different habits at one time. You can't give the same laser-like focus to adopting three new habits rather than one.

Begin with Level 2?

For all of these reasons, it's recommended that you start your changes slowly. In fact, most people who work on this process say that Level 2 is the optimum place to start. Then don't move on to Level 3 until you are positive that you've successfully made your current level a habit.

It's only natural that when you learn a new time management system, you want to use all the steps all at once. That's your natural enthusiasm and zeal kicking in. Containing your enthusiasm and starting and staying with one level until you've mastered it will require quite a bit of patience on your part. But, it won't be overwhelming, either. And actually adopting these steps so they become habits will seem like it takes less effort this way.

For some, actually becoming productive and organized can be an overwhelming struggle. In fact, it's not inaccurate that many individuals feel as if it's a "major life change." Hence, try to make changes gradually, because that way the changes last longer and in some ways become a part of your life. You'll be changing at the most crucial level and far less likely to drop the good habits and run back to the bad within weeks of putting these to the test.

If you're already practicing some of the habits presented here, then start at the level which is most appropriate for your skill level, and then move ahead step by step. This is how you will master your time and achieve your goals.

> *Is what I'm doing or about to do*
> *getting us closer to our objective?*
> — Robert Townsend

Smart Tip to Manage your Time

MAKE TIME TO MEDITATE

How can I find the time to practice meditation daily?

In the desire for spiritual progress, many people decide to sit for at least one hour of meditation, but as soon as they sit down to begin, they remember some work that needs to be done or someone disturbs them and breaks their concentration.

So how do you fix this problem?

One of the solutions is that if you go to work by train, then purchase a first class ticket for yourself. By doing so, you can sit calmly in meditation, without any disturbances until you reach your office.

If you wish to meditate only at home, then set the alarm every day for 4 a.m., sit in meditation for one hour, then go back to sleep. Then wake up again at the usual time. In this way, you have no obstruction to meditation and neither is your schedule disturbed. You can adopt the same idea for exercise.

ENHANCE YOUR ENERGY AND SAVE TIME

Choose the right time of the day

THREE

*What do you buy on spending each day of your life?
Have you ever thought about this?*

We have learnt how to use the three time management levels in order to make the best use of your time and become time-rich. Now let's move on to another important dimension that will help you to become even more time-wealthy.

That dimension is: how to make the highest use of your energy. So, how do you optimize your energy use to save time?

Some individuals believe in attacking and completing the hardest jobs at the start of the day, so you're not expending energy throughout the day trying to figure out a way to keep procrastinating. They believe that if they can get it done at the start of the day, the activity will not burden their mind all day.

Others, though, firmly think that they should start the day off performing the easier activities on their lists. In this way, they'll keep an interest in their work.

The truth of the matter is each person has a different time of the day when they feel the most energetic and active. The bottom line is the amount of energy a person has depends on their nature. But in order to make the most of this productive time, you need to be aware that it exists and then discover approximately what time of the day it is.

> Dr. Mehmet Oz not only performs over 250 heart surgeries a year, but is also a bestselling author and the host of a television show. Dr. Oz doesn't necessarily believe in "time management" as much as he does in "energy management."
>
> According to this theory, you need to stop trying to manage time and instead manage and direct your energies throughout the day. Your goal is to accomplish the most important tasks when your energy level is at its highest.

The cost of movie tickets is a good example of what energy management is all about. If you recall, tickets cost the most on major holidays of the year. Of course, this is because people have more time on these days and usually head for the movies. Even movie-makers target new releases for major holidays. If theater owners know when the energy in their theaters will be the greatest, it shouldn't be too difficult then to determine when you have the most energy to complete what you consider are your roughest tasks.

At a certain point in the day, your energy level is at its highest. You can tell this because you are most enthusiastic and your ability to both think and work is at its best. When you have discovered this, you have learned your most important time of the day.

It only follows then that you shouldn't work at the same pace throughout the day. You should, instead, divide the tasks according to your personal energy levels. For example, most individuals feel the most energetic in the morning. These individuals are probably early risers and like to finish early in the day.

On the other hand are the night owls, those who'd rather stay up late at night and finish their work later in the day. These people say that their best energy levels are in the evening and night. It's at that time of the day when they can accomplish the hardest and largest of the tasks at what seems like a snap of the fingers. It's this time of the day when their concentration is at its highest.

When does your energy level soar? You need to identify your "high-energy time zones." These are the times of the day in which you'll be able to concentrate on activities that you are not extremely interested in, that seem dreary or difficult. "Large tasks" require a larger amount of thinking and energy. Therefore, large tasks and also the ones that simply bore you but are important can also be accomplished during these high-energy zones.

Layers of energy

You probably aren't aware of this, but you, as a human being, possess a tremendous amount of energy. Not only that but you have the ability of using this energy all day long. Simply because you don't realize this, you go through your day, ticking off your tasks with the illusion of a limited amount of energy.

Actually, it's said that you have three levels of energy. The first level you use in the achievement of your daily activities. The second layer is the one you use in case of emergencies. And finally, the third is the layer that few individuals are ever able to access.

Here's a great illustration of what is meant by this.

> A man has used his first level of energy at work. When he finally gets home, he feels exhausted. Then he's invited to a New Year's Eve party that evening. He wants to go and he's infused with a second level of energy. He uses it for partying, singing, and dancing late into the night.

Where did this second round of energy come from? Actually, this energy was always there inside him, which arose and burst forth with the demand that one event made of him. If there had been no party, then more than likely the man never would have tapped that second level of energy. Believe it or not, everyone uses this second layer at some time in their lives.

This now brings us to the third layer of energy, one that you seldom, if ever, use. Regardless of how tired you may be when you go to sleep, if there is a fire somewhere in your house, you would be up all night in a relentless attempt to put it out. When morning comes, you may find that you still have the energy to try and find solutions to the associated problems.

Much in the same way, many individuals use this energy when they go on picnics, plan weddings, and prepare or enjoy other major events. Believe it or not, you can do the same thing, but first you need to be able to identify the inherent energy within you, and then take advantage of it on a daily basis.

Don't wait for events to randomly arise to stir these second, even third levels of energy, to rise to the top. In order to allow that second layer of energy to bubble to the top, you must ignore the first level's initial symptoms of fatigue.

As soon as the lethargy creeps in, don't be oblivious to it. Instead, recognize it and treat it as an opportunity to open the door to the next, second layer of energy. You can do this simply by continuing to work. That's right. Ignore the disinterest and tiredness that's trying to envelop you and instead continue to focus on accomplishing your work. In that way, you'll be able to access a great source of mental strength.

The bottom line is: you must be aware of and identify your own energy. Once you've done this, then you can make great strides in managing your tasks properly with the goal of having a wealth of time and becoming time-rich.

*A river flows and its waters do not come back.
So too, time flows, and the years of your life do not come back.*

– Mahabharata

WORK IS NEVER COMPLETED BY GIVING EXCUSES

Be committed to your work and time

Is not engaging purely in entertainment an expensive investment?

Commitment is a quality which greatly increases the chances of accomplishing a project. It also helps you develop expertise in your work. No organization, company, or person can become proficient in their field without commitment. By being committed to your work and deadlines, you become reliable. Today, there's a great need for reliable people everywhere. These individuals form the core of any company. They are dependable employees and others know they can work with them to forward the goals of the company.

By contrast, those individuals who are unable, for whatever reason, to commit to their work and follow through on their promises are wasting the time of both the company and their fellow workers. This is because they are always giving excuses for not working and not having enough time. Most people agree that it would be better not having these individuals around and instead hire someone new in order to save time and money.

It's only those people who competently complete their work who are given more and greater responsibilities. These confident people who have the ability to stand by their word pave their way to progress and success.

People develop a habit of finding excuses why they couldn't finish their assignments on time. They fail to realize they're only sabotaging themselves when they make excuses. When they discover they can't finish the project on time, they immediately point to situations, issues, or even others for their failure. They try to save themselves from being criticized or blamed, by giving excuses. Due to the fear of disapproval or criticism, they soon begin to habitually device these excuses for their failures.

What these people either don't understand or don't care about is that excuses are the same thing as defeating yourself. These individuals couldn't possibly know how big of a loss they have brought upon themselves, not to mention those they have been working with.

The most astounding part of this entire process is how the individuals who give excuses view the situation. They have no idea that their task sits there unfulfilled and incomplete. They sincerely feel that they have tried their best to complete the work. In their mind, "trying" to complete the task and actually completing it—achieving the final result—are one and the same. They don't understand there's still a gap—sometimes a large canyon—between these two situations.

The following example shows you exactly what we mean.

Your supervisor has requested you to contact a particular individual and relay a message to him. You call the number but the person isn't answering his phone. You may feel that you accomplished your task. You called the individual. The fact that he didn't answer was out of your control.

When your supervisor later asks you about this small assignment, you explain what happened. He said nothing in return and his silence only solidifies your feeling that your task has been sufficiently completed.

What's important here is that "calling the person" and "giving him the message" are two distinctly different things. Technically speaking, "calling the person" is the means by which you are going to accomplish the directive, which in this case is "giving him the message."

This is where you need to honestly ask yourself: "Have I achieved the aim of my task? Have I completed it to get the final result? Did the necessary message reach the person?" Obviously, the answer is a resounding "no." Yes, you did complete the first half of the assignment, but the purpose of that task was to give him the message. If you were honest with yourself, your answer to the questions asked above would be, "No, the work is incomplete."

Reason versus "Realism"

We need to understand that one is a reason and the other is "realism." This may be the first time you're hearing this word, especially in this context. A reason is an excuse a person gives himself as an escape from doing work. A realism, on the other hand, is a cause that is not an excuse, but reality.

Mastering the Art of Time Management | 97

Consider this explanation why a particular assignment couldn't be finished. "I didn't finish because the person with whom I had to work did not come today." Was this a reason or a realism?

Here is one way of understanding the situation. The person you needed to work with was not present today. This person would have come in, had you simply called and explained the importance of their presence today and especially the significance of the timely completion of the project.

If, however, you didn't even try to do this much, it's a good indication that you have provided yourself with an excuse that releases you from any further responsibility. It's in this type of situation, you ask yourself, "Am I my giving myself a reason (that is, an excuse)? Or despite this set of circumstances, can I still complete the assignment?"

Even if after you've called the person, he still doesn't come in, then at least you know you have done everything within your power to complete the task. And that's when there is a "realism" for the job not being completed and not just a reason. In this way, let's take a closer look at the number of tasks you legitimately can't fulfil because of similar "realisms" and you don't need to worry about them.

On the other hand, when looking at reasons or excuses, you will notice there are three main types of reasons:

1. Bad reason

A bad reason is when the concerned person hears and knows that you are giving an excuse to escape doing the work. A man, for example, asks his cook, "What are you cooking for lunch today?"

The cook answers, "I am cooking fish." The master then says, "Wash the fish well before cooking." The cook replies, "Why wash the fish, when it lives in water?!"

This is called a bad reason, which is quite evident to everyone.

2. Big reason

A big reason means you are making big excuses. By giving such excuses, others are easily influenced by what you say. You tell them that you couldn't finish the task because of New Year, a festival, or some other important day has either just occurred or is coming up.

This is usually how this excuse or reason plays out. Someone asks you, why the activity is still not done? You say "Diwali is approaching, so I'm busy. I'll complete it after Diwali." Hearing this explanation, the other person is unable to say anything to you, as you have postponed the job giving a big excuse.

3. Good reason

This is a reason, which you don't believe is an excuse, but if you reflect on it, you will see it is a beautiful excuse. It's due to this type of reason that many of our tasks are left hanging. And because they're left undone, we have an incomplete feeling in our life.

We need to save ourselves from such excuses. For instance, a father says to his son, "Son, please switch off the light." The boy replies, "Father, please close your eyes and you will feel that the light has been switched off." The father says, "Ok Son, please go out and check if it is raining." To this, the boy replies, "Father, the cat is sitting under your bed, please touch it to know if it's raining outside, as it just came in from outside." The father requests, "Son, please at least close the door." The boy snaps, "Why should I do everything?! Why can't you do something?"

The reasons may sound plausible. No one may be able to find anything wrong with them, but finally they are nothing but excuses. The habit of giving such good excuses will be the cause of your failure.

You may feel as if your excuses are very good. They are solid "realisms" why the task is not yet completed. But, before you talk yourself into believing this, ask yourself if it's really necessary to provide an excuse. You can begin by asking yourself this question: "Is the excuse I'm giving true and logical or am I trying to avoid work?"

In other words, you are asking yourself, "Do I have the habit of winning within me?"

The habit of winning

The formula for success is simple:

"Without giving any excuses, work on the job till it's complete."

When you are able to develop this habit, you will begin to achieve true success in your life. Successful people have this habit within them. They are determined to complete every task or job they undertake.

This is because, they believe it's the final result that is ultimately the crucial element to the activity that has been assigned to them. You've probably already heard many examples of this line of thinking. Consider the student who has a burning desire to study, so he studies whenever and wherever he can, even if it means reading under the faint light of the street lamp.

But the stories don't end there, because these are individuals who become engineers, doctors, or astronauts. These are the individuals who end up successful. Successful people refused to give themselves a way out by declaring, "I don't have money to buy books. There's no electricity in my home." They don't make excuses. Instead, they follow through on the task, by working around any obstacle or hurdle. No electricity at home? No problem, I'll find a location with electricity.

The truth of the matter is that those individuals who don't want to do a specific task will find a ton of excuses not to do it. So, you need to ask yourself, "What category do I fall under? Am I someone who gives excuses or the one who sees the job to completion?"

If we revisit the example of the phone call and conveying of the message, do you leave a job half done because of one simple reason? Or do you try repeatedly to call the person until you have reached him and delivered the message?

Similarly, what would you do if someone asked you to get something from a particular store? You go to the store they requested, but when you get there, it's closed. Truthfully, what would be your next step? Would you search for another shop where you could purchase the same item in an attempt to conclude the job?

If you're not used to completing tasks with any regularity, then begin by tackling the small ones. By doing so, you'll be increasing your confidence and your willpower. It will also increase your ability to move on to larger, more complex tasks and complete these eventually.

Soon, you'll discover that you will be able to fulfill every promise you make to others without the need to give any "reason" or excuse why the task isn't done. That, in turn, means your attribute of "commitment" is developing and growing by leaps and bounds. But that's not all. Your work too will be completed in a planned manner and within the estimated time span.

If you have made the decision that you will exercise a minimum of four days a week, then you must stick to that schedule. When you provide yourself with no excuse, then you will definitely make the time for it. Of course, you can find a thousand reasons not to exercise: you've got guests at home, you're tired due to heavy workload, you woke up late this morning and can't spare the time… should we continue?

But when you are determined to follow through and stick with your plan, then you give yourself no choice but to exercise even if it's only for a short fifteen minutes.

You would be surprised at how many individuals are actually afraid of making promises or resolutions, because they believe that they may not be able to fulfill them. If they don't fulfill them, they feel guilty and disappointed. But worse than that, they lose their self-confidence.

However, when you stand by your word, you will see that people begin to place their trust in you, and your self-confidence, in turn, expands.

> A disciple once asked his master, "I'm studying for the twelfth grade at school and I cannot find time to sit in meditation. How can I find the time?" His master responded with a question, "What time do you wake up

in the morning?" He replied, "7 o'clock." The master said, "Wake up daily at 7, but tell your mind you woke up at 7:15."

The student failed to understand this line of reasoning. The master explained, "If you get up one hour late on a particular day, then that one hour has been wasted. In the same way, when you wake up at 7 and sit in meditation for 15 minutes, you can imagine you didn't get up until 7:15. By doing so, you'll be able to meditate. You'll also save yourself from making excuses."

In this way, you will become a disciplined person—one who is not easily swayed by excuses. To become truly disciplined, you have to look within and ask yourself honestly, "Is the excuse I'm giving a reason or a realism? Am I saying this because it's the truth or because I don't want to do this activity?"

If your answer is, "The task must be completed," then you need to follow through on that, regardless of the difficulty level and the challenges it presents. When gold is tempered in fire, it becomes pure because it has endured much hardship. Similarly, if you resolve to complete your work without giving any excuses, then with the passage of time, you, too, will shine just like gold and become pure. Completing a task gives you a good feeling and a sense of completion and fulfilment. And that's what makes you time-wealthy.

Ninety-nine percent of the failures come from people who have the habit of making excuses.

– George Washington Carver

GIVE TIME FOR INCOMPLETE WORK

Self-suggestions for time

It is important to ask: What do I want to achieve today? 1. Nothing; 2. Everything; 3. Something; 4. A lot; 5. Control.

One of the vital aspects of time and work management is the crucial influence your thoughts, feelings, and intentions play in your success. We've alluded to this previously, but it's so important that it's worth explaining further.

Regardless of the tasks you perform as part of your daily routine, you have already assigned a thought or a feeling to them. Feelings are, of course intangible and you can't see them, so they are difficult for some of us to understand.

Here's what we mean, though. If you believe the task that you're working on at the moment is difficult, that you can't possibly complete it on time, that it's boring, then these feelings contribute to the job being boring and not getting completed on time.

When it comes to time and work management, individuals usually focus solely from an impartial perspective. And sometimes this is exactly what trips them up in not being successful. They fail to be aware that their emotions, however obscured and buried deep beneath their surface, are pivotal elements in their success.

In essence, they're tackling the process backwards. Yes! Before they can rein in the time element, they must realize and act on the basic premise that each task evokes an emotion within us and is a major influence in how we approach and complete it.

You first must work on identifying the underlying emotions associated with each activity before you could possibly save any time. Specifically, you need to change those negative thoughts and emotions you've attached to the job into positive ones that will promote a quicker turnaround as well as make the job if not pleasant to work on, but at least not that much of a burden.

When you wake up in the morning, you think, "Today feels like a lazy day. I really don't think I'll be able to complete any work." The odds are that's exactly what's going to happen. If you have any hope of salvaging the day, then you need to find a way of turning your thoughts around. You need to consciously say to yourself, "Today, I'm bringing important tasks to completion." You can also say something along the lines of: "I am feeling fully active and energetic, so there are no obstacles that can prevent me from completing my work today."

The key in changing your routine for the better is changing your thoughts and then approaching your work with a new energetic attitude. Many individuals fail to change their thoughts because they don't realize how important thoughts are in improving their productivity.

You hear it a lot: "Change your thoughts." In response, you may question why having positive thoughts actually matters. It is, though, only when you actually try it that you'll experience the joy of the results. The transformation occurs in the part of yourself that is not seen by the eye. This means, the moment you begin to change your thoughts, you set up a series of events, invisible at first, but which will create a chain reaction that will soon reveal itself.

Where do you begin working on your time management improvements? Start with a simple intention. You may want to promise yourself that this week you will spend less time watching television or you will not waste your time (and that of others) with unnecessary talk.

When you set intentions in this manner, you'll see that automatically your focus actually shifts away from watching television or idle talk. All you need to do is, start with one simple intention. From there, your courage and faith grows, and eventually so will your intentions. This, in turn, will steer your life to a brand new, successful direction.

You may be saying right now that you've tried all this before, why should this attempt be any different? Because in this attempt, you will have some ready-made affirmations to begin reciting when you feel yourself slipping.

Repeat positive affirmations

Let's start right now. What negative thoughts do you hold regarding time? Now take these negative thoughts and rephrase these as positive ones. Below are some examples of positive self-suggestions.

1. I am complete; all my tasks are completed on time.
2. Time is my friend; it supports me generously.

3. Since time is abundant, all my jobs are completed on time.
4. I am skilled at time management.
5. I impressively manage all the areas of my life.
6. Managing time is easy for me.
7. I am committed in a remarkable manner towards the management of my time.
8. My time and my life are in my control.
9. I am a good organizer and always pay attention to time.
10. I manage time smoothly and naturally.

Feel free to choose any of the positive affirmations above in order to counter your negative thoughts. If none of these appeals to you, then create your own. As you repeat these throughout the day, be sure to connect your faith and feelings with the affirmations. Repeat them as often as you need to until they are absorbed by your system and are revealed through your behavior.

Importance of the feeling of completion

Let's consider an example.

> A student approached his master with a problem. "Master, I begin my work with passion but after a while my enthusiasm fades, and then I leave those jobs incomplete. Why does this happen?"
>
> The Master said, "Keep reminding yourself with what feeling and intention you began your work. When you are able to see those clearly once more, then your energy

will again rise and your work will be completed. At the same time, think about why you developed the tendency of losing enthusiasm in the first place. If you identify the root of this tendency, you will be liberated from it."

Think about it for a minute. There is not a single person who really wants to leave their work unfinished. That's why it's so important that you develop the habit of always finishing your work. When you ask yourself questions, like the one the Master suggested to his student, then you can strengthen your resolve to complete your work. Don't worry that you may not find an immediate answer. It's not an easy question to answer, to be truthful.

Contemplate for some time. What specific tasks in your life you haven't been able to accomplish till date? It's imperative that you see all of your activities to completion after you take them on. Work is worship. It's not a burden or merely a responsibility. Always keep this in mind.

Do you have the habit of going to bed at night with your tasks in varying stages of incompletion? If your answer is yes, then you should think about creating a rule that you will ask yourself this simple question every night: *"What small task can I complete now, before I sleep?"*

As soon as you ask this question, you will remember a few small activities, like returning objects to their proper places, reading or sending a few emails, sending someone a message on the phone, preparing your school or office things for the next day. You may also remember that you had wanted to soak pulses for the following day or even take two minutes to meditate or pray.

If you take care of only a few of these things before turning in for the night and save yourself even five minutes out of your day tomorrow, that is a start toward even greater savings as you continue with this process. While doing this, you find that the small activities are now complete. You have taken vital steps in developing a habit that will later become invaluable when you are in the process of completing larger activities.

You are going to experience completeness only after completing your jobs. If you don't follow through on them, you'll be filled with a sense of incompleteness or even despondency till the very end of your life.

Regardless of how many jobs one accomplishes, most people on their deathbed feel they have left some job incomplete or undone. So, please understand the importance of finishing each job while you are alive and kicking, so you can experience satisfaction in your life.

Ever notice that when you have incomplete jobs hovering over you, there are accompanying thoughts racing through your head, which refuse to let you get a moment's rest? Despite your best intentions, your mind flits between the past and the future. It's unable to stay in the present. These are the thoughts that tend to drain a lot of your time and energy. And you find yourself in a position where you aren't able to accomplish any work nor do you feel the desire to start anything new.

The mind flies to the past. There is something unfinished which pulls at it continually. As soon as you remember something, your mind says, "I wish I would have done this thing… I should have said this or that to someone… I wish I would have completed this course because I would have a better job right now…"

When you begin to think in this manner, you will see many items in your life, starting from your childhood up to the present moment, which are incomplete and refuse to leave you. You wander through life carrying these burdens with you. Because of the accumulation of these incomplete activities, your mind is cooking up imaginary tales like Sheikh Chilli: "I will achieve my desires in this manner... My work will be completed in this way... If I do this, then everything will be perfect..."

You cannot experience the satisfaction of completeness in the present moment because your mind is always running in the past or the future. It's only when you achieve completeness in the here and now that you'll have nowhere to go.

Starting an activity has its own importance. But completing that activity is equally important. Those individuals who take a job and complete it are those who are growing and progressing in life.

That's why it's crucial that starting today you finish as many tasks as you can that are cluttering your mind by sitting around undone.

> *A man who dares to waste one hour of time*
> *has not discovered the value of life.*
>
> *– Charles Darwin*

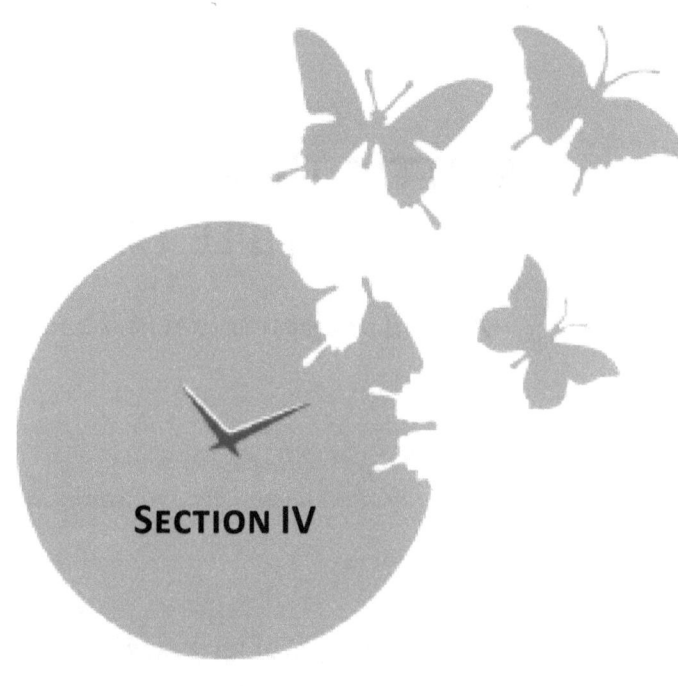

Section IV

SMALL SAVINGS OF TIME

A LITTLE TIME CAN BENEFIT MULTIPLE TASKS

A small but power-packed beginning

*Aim for 1% more
than what seems like a realistic goal.*

Just as the ocean is made of up of tiny drops of water, time is composed of little moments of every day. You can become time-rich simply by harvesting or saving these tiny portions of time. A way to do this is by achieving the completion of several jobs by giving them each a small amount of time every day.

Far too often, you may feel overwhelmed by the large amount of tasks you have to accomplish in a seemingly small amount of time. If you're like many others, you ask yourself, "I have so much work, how can I possibly work on so many different tasks at the same time?"

While you're working on an important and urgent project, it's difficult and sometimes impossible, to pay attention simultaneously to another equally important and urgent project. You are in the midst of multiple responsibilities on one project and, quite understandably, you're not able to give time to any other work. It makes you feel helpless. Instead of wasting your energy in feeling "out of control," you need to channel this energy toward managing time. Then you will be able to make time even for the other important tasks on your list.

As you may recall from our earlier discussion, many individuals aren't able to start their work because they are too busy. Too busy waiting for the desire, mood, or feeling to strike them. Until that time, they procrastinate, expecting that the perfect moment will appear at any time. Of course, what these individuals need to do is not wait for the desire, but realize that "feelings follow action." *This means action and feelings advance side by side.*

Once you begin to regulate your work, i.e. work on a project whether or not you like it, then your feelings will automatically fall in line and regularize as well. Start the task and you'll then discover that the desire wells up inside of you to complete it. You need not coax or cajole it. The actual performance is the locus of our control in the process. The eliciting of the feeling is not. So, if you were to wait for that desire, that feeling, you could be waiting for an indefinite time, knowing that these are aspects of work that you simply cannot predict or keep under control.

You now understand why it's crucial that you abandon the idea of waiting for inspiration to strike you to begin work. Instead, just buckle up and begin regardless of your mood. That's easier said than done, many people counter. Yes, sometimes it certainly does seem that way. The following is a technique that can help you with this.

Secret of accomplishing a big responsibility: A little, but today

You've probably heard of the adage "Little drops of water make the mighty ocean." It's a similar message that suits this situation excellently.

As you begin your work, remind yourself that by accomplishing even a little a day, it's possible to complete a big project. Even within a space of 5-10 minutes, you'll see that the important job will be progressing relentlessly toward completion.

In much the same way, Indian freedom fighter and social reformer Bal Gangadhar Tilak devoted a bit of time every day to writing while he was in prison and finished *The Gita Rahasya*. He did not wait for the mood to strike him. He simply wrote a little every day. The same can be said of the social activist and author Sane Guruji, who gave only small but consistent chunks of time and finished writing *Shyamchi Aai*. This book is hailed as one of the greatest tributes to mother's love in Marathi literature.

Neither of these individuals waited, hoping the right place, mood, or time would descend upon them to put their pen to paper and begin to write. Instead, they used whatever time and place was available and just wrote.

Suppose you think, "I don't have time today. I'm not in the mood to do that today." By thinking so, you've already killed your productivity for the day. Instead, you should be asking yourself, "Despite the fact that I don't have the time and I'm not in the mood, can I at least devote 10 minutes to this project?" You'll be amazed at how often the answer is yes and some minor aspect of it will be completed. This is how you invest, bit by bit, the time necessary to achieve the completion of other important projects on your list as well.

You must realize that even when you give seemingly inconsequential time periods to an important project on a regular basis, it propels you closer to its completion. To help you remember this when you are in the grips of an overwhelming workload, just recite the mantra: "A little, but today." This is a very effective affirmation and will ensure the continuity and eventual completion of your work.

As human beings, we seem to have a burning desire for great achievements. The only problem with that is, we seldom know the best way to take it all the way to realization. Many individuals have applied it and believe this short and concise mantra is a big secret to success.

If you believe that this mantra is an excellent time management tool, then you should also consider the importance of the other affirmations sprinkled throughout this book that are equally useful. Make the decision today that you will start using the affirmations, even if it be in small measures. The key is to begin right now.

You may be familiar with the proverb that "you can eat an elephant as long as it's cut into small enough pieces." This means that the thought of eating an elephant may be overwhelming, given its enormity. However, if it's cut up into small segments, you can eat it.

Regardless of how large of a responsibility your project is and the expanse of its size, you don't have to feel overwhelmed looking at it in its entirety. Instead, visualize it in smaller pieces. Dissect it so you are only seeing the small bits. Even the most difficult, complicated, and largest pieces of your project can be accomplished if pulled apart piece by piece. Instead of trying to accomplish a big assignment or responsibility all at once, you must break it down and address it bit by bit.

Think about how this can apply in all sorts of ways in your life:

- If you wish to read a book, then you may decide to read one chapter daily.
- If you wish to write a book, then you may decide to write one page daily.
- If you wish to clean your house, then you may decide to clean one corner daily.

After some time, you will be pleasantly surprised that many of your tasks have been completed.

Why not start today? Begin by observing your thoughts, actions, habits—both good and bad—as well as your behavior. Accomplish a little, but do it today.

A little bit more

"A little bit more" means by doing a small amount on a daily basis, increase your capacity of performing your work. If you have studied for an hour, for example, you start feeling tired. At this point, you stop, because you believe you have done a lot.

Instead, you should be asking yourself, "Can I work just another five minutes?" If your answer is no, then say to yourself, "I'm doing this work for the enrichment of my qualities and for my self-expression." You'll notice an immediate change in your behavior and you will be able to work for five more minutes. In this way, you can raise your capacity to work. By maintaining that same outlook in all endeavors in your life, then you, slowly but surely, will bring about great changes.

Accomplishing even one task that aligns with your goals is akin to watering a seed every day. If you work consistently at it just a little on a daily basis, then one day your goal will have been reached without you ever realizing it. By watering that small seedling daily, the next thing you know, you'll have an enormous, resplendent tree standing in front of you. This tree will provide you with the necessary shade. And as a bonus, it becomes the source of an abundant delicious fruit too.

If you have work to do, don't wait to feel like it; set to work and you will feel like it."

— Henry James, Roderick Hudson

THE TWO-MINUTES TECHNIQUE

The magic of minutes

The Awareness Rule:
You must be completely present in the work while doing it.
(Mindfulness, Remindfulness, Playfulness)

How much time does procrastination cost you in a typical day? The tasks and activities that you delay doing, occupy much of your time—time that could have been invested in other activities.

The following is an effective technique to deal with this problem. When you use it, you'll be saving your time today and ensuring you're not losing it on future issues. This method is best understood when explained in two parts.

Part 1: If any task takes two minutes or less, then do it immediately.

As stated by David Allen in his book *Getting Things Done*, it helps to immediately address those tasks that won't take more than two minutes. Surprisingly, the activities you put off for another time very often take two minutes or less. It's true. A great example of such a task is placing the items you use daily back in their proper places. Another less-than-two-minute task could be sending a simple email.

Similarly, this idea usually holds for the chores around the house. It doesn't normally take any more than a few minutes to fold clothes and put them away in the closet, or clean a table that has things scattered all over it. Even answering a simple, short question can usually be completed within two minutes. Why not pick up the phone and answer that voice mail with a short two-minute answer?

Think about it. None of these activities take more than two minutes to accomplish, but yet, if you're like most of us, you try your hardest to ignore them. The problem is that the longer you ignore them, the larger the task grows. Soon, it has grown into an activity that may take more than two minutes.

The first part of this secret is the two-minute limit of the task. You must make the decision to execute right now—or face a larger project later. That's when you face a task you certainly can groan while doing it. Hence, before you procrastinate yet another task, simply ask yourself this question: *"How much time will it take me to complete this?"*

If the answer is "one or two minutes," then conclude the task right there and then. In this way, you can break free of the habit of procrastination.

Another brief question that can put you on track in two minutes is: *"How can I make the best use of my time at this moment?"* This is a great question to ask yourself throughout the day.

So, that was the first part of this incredibly insightful technique. Once you've started using this principle, try the second part of the technique.

Part 2: When you are cultivating a new habit, it should take less than two minutes of your time

Can all of your goals be achieved in two minutes? You'd say, of course not. You would've not only scoffed at that notion, but laughed. But if asked, can every goal be started by working on it for two minutes? You would most probably say, why not?

The truth of the matter is, those who have actually achieved their aspirations must have started someplace. And it could very well be that they started with a little step. If you wish to achieve your aspirations, then you simply need to take the first step toward it today.

In order to develop any habit and achieve your goal, it's important to begin. After beginning, it's important to do it consistently. Many times, it's not so important how you did the job. What's important is cultivating a habit of working on it. Once you develop this habit, you'll notice that as you continue, you have become proficient in it.

When you put the two-minute technique to work for you, then you'll see that the process is actually more important than the result of the activity. This amazing technique is extremely valuable for those people to whom going through the process is even more important than the goal itself. The central point of this technique is to begin the task and then keep it going consistently

The next time you're trying to develop a new habit, ask yourself one question: "What can I do that would take two minutes or less to execute?" If you're thinking about making exercise a regular part of your day, then you may want to start by asking, "What kind of exercise would take me only two minutes or less?" You may decide that any smaller section of your body can be exercised in this amount of time, like your neck, eyes, or hands. If that's the case, then you can start right away and then slowly increase the time you devote to your new program.

This two-minute technique was originally discovered by Isaac Newton. If you recall, one of his laws of physics is: "An object at rest stays at rest and an object in motion stays in motion with the same speed and in the same direction unless acted upon by an unbalanced force." The same way that this law applies to objects, it applies to humans as well.

Once you begin to take action toward your goal, you will discover that you want to continue it. Don't think that this technique is useful for just smaller goals. It's a valuable method for your larger goals, dreams, and aspirations as well. Some people have trouble starting any activity, but once they actually begin it, then with consistency they have no trouble continuing it and eventually completing it. Below are just some examples of how you can put this technique into practice.

- If you wish to develop the habit of eating healthy food, then begin by eating just one fruit. Even one fruit a day will motivate you to eat healthy food.
- If you wish to begin reading, then begin by reading just one page daily.
- If you wish to begin writing, then begin by writing just two lines daily.
- If you wish to begin taking a stroll early in the morning, then begin by walking on your terrace or a big room for two minutes daily.

Through the sincere practice of the two-minute technique, you will be able to save time and energy, and before you know it, you would be time-rich.

Smart Tip to Master your Time

WHAT AM I GOING TO COOK TODAY?

Is a lot of your time spent in thinking over this question?

Research states that most women experience high stress levels every day as they try to decide what they should prepare for each meal.

There's an easy solution. Simply dedicate 40 minutes in a month for this activity. During this time, sit with a notebook and cookbook to create a list of the family meals for the month. You might even want to use a computer or laptop or even your mobile phone for this purpose. In this way, you can avoid the daily stress of deciding the menu and, in the process, save time that could otherwise be invested in other tasks.

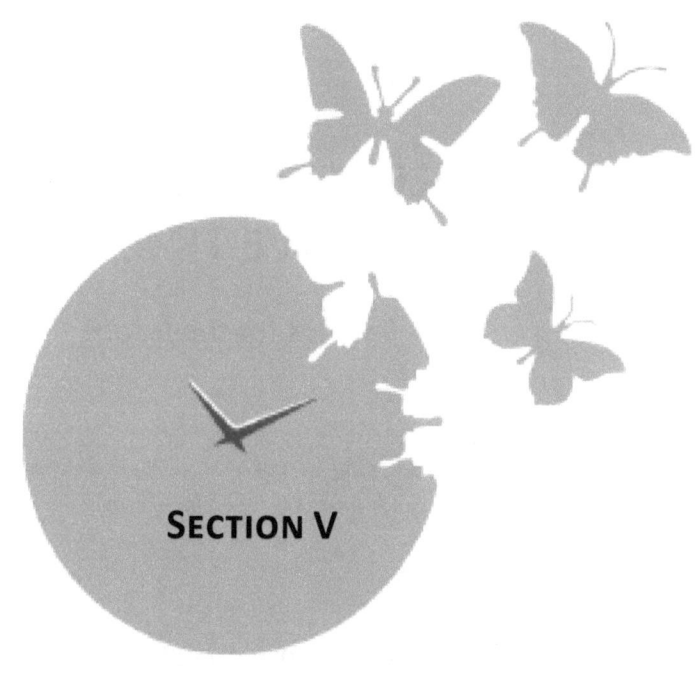

SECTION V

HUGE SAVINGS OF TIME

DELEGATE TASKS AND SAVE TIME

Savings for the future

*Avoid being part of other people's dramas.
It will save you a lot of time.*

If you are overwhelmed at work to the point that you can no longer honor your obligations, then you may find yourself seeking an assistant. Before you do this, consider these words of caution.

Don't find people to only "do the work." Instead, seek capable people for the position—whatever position you're filling. If you discover you can't find a capable person, then choose a good candidate and "empower" them. In other words, train that person to become capable.

Delegating tasks to others is not something everyone finds easy to do. Many individuals are confused, faced with notions and beliefs, which hinder their ability to let go and trust another person to perform a task. Do you too find it difficult sometimes because you are worried it won't be carried out as well as you could? Or perhaps you are fearful that the assignment won't get completed on time.

The truth of the matter is, though, that once you've learned how to delegate, this one trait can save you an immense amount of time. For some time management experts, the concept of "delegating work" is even more important an ability than "saving time."

Before we go any further in this discussion, you should understand this fully in order to save large chunks of time for yourself every day.

Do you feel nervous every time a deadline for a task or project looms? Do you feel work is more of a burden than a blessing? In spite of all this, do you still find it difficult to pass off or delegate an activity to a surrogate? If so, then you need to review how work is delegated and prepare yourself to do exactly that.

Just as you are learning to become a trustworthy person, you should be giving that opportunity to others too. The first step in delegating is to find someone you feel comfortable with and give them a chance to prove that they are a trustworthy and reliable person as well. It's in this way they can expand and discover all the potential they have inside them.

One of the reasons you would rather not do this is because you feel the process is overwhelming. First, you're investing time to train them. This alone makes some people sigh. It's not unusual to find that many people think that in the time it takes to train someone, it would be easier to tackle the activity themselves. Then there's the corner of our ego that keeps whispering to us that no one but you can perform the activity and give it the justice it deserves.

If you have a presentation to give, then you would rather prepare for it on your own. After all, you understand the topic well and in detail. It would be near to impossible, you reason, to delegate this to anyone else without investing time in explaining everything to them and telling them what kind of presentation you expect. According to this line of thinking, you would sum it up as a huge waste of time.

Businessman, author, and speaker Dave Ramsey has said, "Delegation requires the willingness to pay for short term failures in order to gain long term competency." Therefore, let's look at the same example from a slightly different perspective. It can ultimately end up being a huge time saver. How could this be?

Consider the two benefits of training someone to help you, listed below:

1. When you invest your time in training an assistant, you can then invest your expertise in developing better strategies, or improving or elaborating on the presentation.

2. You also become the source of the advancement of skill and capacity in others. The next time you assign them another crucial task, you will need to invest less time and they would do a better job.

When you delegate work to others, you provide them an opportunity to use their full capabilities toward their progress and toward collaboration. As a result, you save time.

Richard Branson, the founder of the *Virgin Group* which controls more than 400 companies, believes that he's been able not only to get out of the office more often, but actually accomplish more critical work because he is able to delegate much of his work. He believes that communicating verbally with people is of far more importance than just replying and corresponding on email. By delegating work, he is able to invest his time in meeting and getting to know more people. Additionally, the time that he saves, he devotes to exercising and in writing his thoughts down. He is an author of international bestsellers and a renowned philanthropist.

Prepare your representative

If you are going to follow through and find a person you can delegate a portion of your work to, then you must prepare him/her for this assignment. In effect, you are not only preparing an assistant, but in the best case scenario, you are training your representative. Your representative is a person who you have full confidence in to act on your behalf.

Typically, you'll discover that you will delegate the activity to be completed by explaining the process and the corresponding responsibility verbally. But this is not always a foolproof method and many times not an effective way of training. It's far better, at the same time you are directing this person verbally, to have some type of written instructions he could turn to should he need them. You can see immediately how this small addition in the training process can help reduce mistakes and misunderstandings immensely.

With only verbal instructions, it's possible that either he didn't recall the instructions exactly as you gave them or didn't understand their full intended meaning. In either case, after a while he forgot some aspects of the activity. If he had written instructions, then he could easily double-check and see for himself where he's getting confused, before the small mistakes accumulate and build into something more serious.

Below are the vital steps you need to take when you are delegating activities to your representative. If you must, take a pen and paper and rewrite these, so you can understand them more fully.

1. Make a list of your employees and make 5 columns after each name.

2. Against their name in the first section, write down their qualities and talents, those talents specifically that are necessary for the accomplishment of the task. If an individual, for example has been charged with the task of creating the cover of a book, then mention in the column that he has graphic design skills or experience in creating book covers. Similarly, if you're delegating tasks related to accounting, then mention this skill or his experience in this area in the column.

3. The next section should be labeled "Important Tasks." Here you mention the vital activities already assigned to this individual. If, for example, you have asked someone to draw up a production plan, then note this in the "important tasks" column next to the person's name.

4. The third column will be for the "time limit." This is the most important column. If the task entrusted to your employee has no stipulated completion date, then it will never get done. When there's a date assigned to the goal, only then the goal becomes more precise and explicit.

Let's say that someone takes on a goal related to health. They, then, need to ask themselves this question: "What is my health-related goal?" If they answer saying "I want to be healthy," then this is not a concrete goal. In fact, it's vague and open to interpretation on when the task has been accomplished—if it can ever be achieved fully.

It's much better to say, "I want to lose 5 kg." In this way, you have a marker to reach for. When you have lost those 5 kilograms, then you can set yourself another goal, every bit as precise and explicit as this one.

You need to do something similar when you are assigning goals to your representatives. You assign one individual, for example, with the task of "making phone calls all day in order to generate prospective customers." What kind of goal is that? It's undefined and not in the least bit clear.

This scenario could very well end in disaster. If, at the end of the day, you ask your representative how many people he called, you may not get the response you were expecting. He may reply that he called five people but not a single one of them answered the phone.

It's at this point that you may doubt the method you used to delegate this task. If the goal of the activity was to secure prospective customers, how could this ever be achieved at this rate? Instead, you should have assigned this person a specific and concrete goal. "You must contact and speak with at least 15 people daily. You may discover that you need to call 30-40 individuals just to talk to those 15. If that's the case, it's fine."

Researchers conducted a study to understand the importance of tying a specific completion time to an assigned task. A group of participants was called to a playground and told, "Begin running laps around the playground. When you're tired, let us know." A second group was also asked to run laps around the same playground. They were told, however, to run ten laps.

The results proved quite interesting. The first group ran an average of five laps before they told the researchers they were unable to run anymore. Meanwhile, the second group had completed their ten laps.

What's the difference? You guessed it. The first group had no real goal. They were just to go out there and run. The second group, by contrast, were instructed to run a specific number of laps with no loophole that if before they reached the tenth lap they could quit if they got tired.

And there's the vivid difference between a set goal and imprecise instructions.

The next time you're assigning tasks to your representatives, you'll probably be thinking about this study and assign clear and precise goals to go with them. The key to assigning an understandable, reachable goal is by focusing not on the execution of the task itself, but on its final result. What do you want to see come out of this activity? Only then will you be able to see the goals being realized.

5. You'll label the fourth column "Agreement." Here, you and your representative agree after discussing the nature of the task to complete the work that has been assigned to them. Don't be surprised if you have employees who don't want to do what you assign them. They assume the responsibility only because you insist. Since they felt they were without options, they reluctantly and half-heartedly accept the assignment. For this very reason, they never really

felt as if they consented to the task and feel as if they have no responsibility for it being fully completed.

While you're discussing the need to agree on what needs to be done, also talk to your representative to see that they also agree with the process. Should they have questions or perhaps suggestions, this would be a great time to talk about them. Be sure they are in agreement with what is expected of them. Do they understand the possible obstacles they could be faced with? Do they fully understand the full responsibilities involved in the activity? Make sure you both know where each of you stands in regard to the process and completion of the task.

6. You'll label the fifth column "Feasibility." This means you need to also check to ensure that completing the assignment is even possible. The best determination of this is by asking yourself the following question: "If this were assigned to me, would I be able to accomplish it?" If the answer is "yes," then you can feel relatively confident the person you are assigning it to will also be able to complete it. When delegating the work to the individual, make sure you emphasize to him that after careful consideration you believe it's an achievable task. At this time, the two of you can also talk in detail about the process and procedures that need to be used in order to accomplish it fully. In this way, you are ensuring that your representative has both an interest in the activity as well as the motivation to see it to completion.

By following the steps mentioned in this chapter, you'll be able to easily delegate and complete the many assignments that flow across your desk daily. But after you have assigned the work, your responsibilities in regard to the assignment aren't quite fulfilled. Once the work is returned to you, take the time to review it. Make sure that it's done to your specifications.

Accept it as completed only if it has been accomplished well and meets your standards. If it doesn't, then return it to the person who worked on it to improve it. Don't worry that you're being strict or "mean." This is the only way your representative will gain the necessary knowledge on accomplishing the task properly. This allows them, in the long run, to increase their accuracy and efficiency.

When your representative accomplishes a task well, don't forget to show your appreciation. You must thank them and thank them sincerely. You have a responsibility to develop not only the habit of showing your gratitude for a job well done, but also occasionally rewarding them. It's only in this way that the two of you will begin to trust each other. It's also nice to be appreciated for performing well. You will not only be establishing a professional relationship built on trust, but you will be helping your representative gain confidence in his work and himself.

The delegation of assignments is not just a part of your job. If done correctly, delegation is actually an art. At its best, it provides you and your representative with an opportunity to progress and enjoy a victory. Considering all this, you can feel confident in assigning work to others, knowing it will be completed to your specifications.

And when you can do, you open up an entirely new dimension of time for yourself.

SAVE TIME WITH THE POWER OF YOUR THOUGHTS

Four Aspects of New Thinking

*By telling your thoughts "later" or "next,"
you can return to the present,
connect with your task at hand, and save time.*

We all know how powerful thoughts are—both negative and positive. But few people fully understand the enormous benefits thoughts can have over the management of your time in your everyday life. Before you can truly be proficient at time management, you need to be familiar with the four aspects of the incredible power of thoughts.

Aspect 1 of Power of Thoughts

Individuals tasked with vital or crucial roles, should take a pause for a few moments from time to time, to reflect and reassess their work.

This means you should take occasional breaks from your work to detach and take a refreshed look at your work. The idea behind this habit is simple yet one few persons talk about. It is a fact that you must invest some time to contemplate whether you should continue working in the same manner as you always have, or you need to rethink over it. You may discover that you need to make some changes or adjust your approach somewhat.

There are times when it's necessary to pause and view your work from a slightly different perspective. This will enable you to actually see what you've been doing, otherwise you may continue to work in the same way mechanically—even if it's beneficial or not.

Many individuals stubbornly refuse to take these short breaks from their work, fearful that if they pause, they'll lose that time that they should be working on the task at hand. But it's more vital to take a break for the best accomplishment of your work—both in the matter of time and in the quality of your actions.

You should learn how to take time out for contemplation. When you start this, you'll immediately notice that you will be making much quicker progress on your project. In effect, you will actually be saving time using this "secret."

Are you serious about expanding your time, and in the process saving large chunks of time? Then ask yourself the following question: "What are the specific activities or habits that waste much of my time?"

Let's say that a person is spending his time every day moving his diary, pen, and the rest of his stationery from one room to another for his regular writing sessions. If he were to move his diary to the spot where he habitually sits every day, he could save much time and energy (not to mention saving him from becoming frustrated).

Yes, you're right. This is a small and simple example, but there are several such small activities that eventually eat away large chunks of your day. The power of thought tells us: If you bring your attention to such things and make small changes, it soon adds into large savings of time.

It is essential, then, that we continually review the task at hand. As time passes, we gain new insight into the work. With the passage of time, you may also discover that you gain new information from unexpected sources. You may even find new people getting associated with you, who may open up different aspects of your work.

As you progress in your work, you may also see a new position emerge. You may move onto a different role. Simultaneously, your most important task becomes teaching the work and the dynamics of the job to someone else whom you'll eventually be assigning this work to.

Surprisingly, this avenue had not been available to you earlier, so there was no way you could follow it previously. But this means that eventually someone will be able to take your place, leaving you the option of involving yourself in a different activity, a project you've been wanting to embrace for a while, but couldn't find the time for it.

When contemplating your work, you must think on all its various aspects. If a new aspect comes to mind, you should try it out. Perhaps you see a different way of performing a task that may save you time and effort.

You can decide a definite time period for yourself, say every three months or six months or a year, after which you will rethink over everything you are doing in a new and creative manner.

Aspect 2 of Power of Thoughts

While traveling along your journey toward a new and better life, it's vital to your success that you continue to keep an attitude of foresight.

Foresight is the ability to look ahead and "see" what could take place in the future. It's a habit that can save you much time in the future. For example, your body is sending you some signals of uneasiness. Perhaps, it's an occasional pain. In this case, if you could use your foresight, you will understand that these sort of problems may increase as part of the natural aging of the body, however, you don't want it to turn into a chronic problem. To avoid your pain from getting to that state, you institute an exercise program starting today. When you receive the indication for health, it means you must take a minimum of one minute out of your day to exercise, one minute for *pranayama* or controlled breathing exercises, one minute of contemplation, and one minute on silent meditation.

Increase the time on these practices in increments of one minute every week or according to the schedule you've set for them.

The key to success in this case is not to wait around for your pain to return. Instead, use this ritual when you first feel unease, and then continue with it, regardless of how you've been feeling.

Unfortunately, there are very few people who can truly be called "farsighted." There are individuals who practice foresight and are able to see far enough in the future based on what's happening in the world today. They can imagine what will happen, say, ten years from now. Once they can see that, they then legitimately ask themselves what they need to do today in order for them to avoid the difficulties that can occur and thereby lead a good and happy life in the future. Once they are confident what needs to be done, they start working toward it right from today.

When you maintain your foresight and act on it, you will clearly find that in the future most individuals will complain about the challenges and troubles they are facing. You will, however, discover that you won't be one of them. Instead, you can be pleased that you had used your foresight, and not only anticipated the problem but also found a solution to it. This not only saved you time trying to adjust and solve problems at this time but also enabled you to make your life smoother and easier.

The beauty of using foresight is that you can anticipate a problem in the future, but you don't allow yourself to worry about in the present moment. When you've armed yourself with foresight, you have effectively armed yourself with logic and sound judgment. You begin to use the present time effectively and efficiently, leading to a bright future.

Aspect 3 of Power of Thoughts

When you're listening to something important, try to grasp even the subtle things that are being told, and reflect deeply on them. Contemplate also on the aspects that you have observed.

When you choose to contemplate in this manner, your thoughts become crystal clear and even the minutest areas are much easier to fully understand and grasp. Those individuals who are capable of discovering and then concentrating on the deepest and most subtle aspects of concepts are those who will be experiencing the most changes in their life for the better.

But the benefits don't end there. This habit enables you to become capable of achieving the biggest and highest goals. You are easily able to progress on the path of development. You will be blessed with new possibilities and fresh opportunities. These situations will unfold with little effort on your part. By seeing and realizing these potential possibilities on time, you are able to use your time in the best manner to explore those possibilities and make the best of the opportunities. It's up to you now to continue this practice of deep and subtle reflection, regardless of the results you receive.

Aspect 4: Out-of-the-box thinking

Out-of-the-box thinking means breaking away from the prison of the old patterns of looking at things.

With this kind of thinking, you'll break free of the old thinking—out of the box as it were—and emerge with new and exciting ways of viewing things. A person who brings an "out-of-the-box" attitude to the problem will likely find a completely new way of doing things.

This type of thinking practically guarantees that something new will come into existence, thanks to a total change in your thoughts. You'll find that you approach the problem or task with a refreshingly open mind.

Out-of-the-box thinking also gives birth to a dazzlingly amazing array of new possibilities. So, how do you even begin to think out-of-the-box? It's easier to provide an example than to try to explain it.

> A father bought a watermelon for his two sons. Both brothers love this fruit and are very happy to see it. The older brother offers to cut the watermelon. The father

agrees. The boy thinks, "This is great. I'll cut a large piece for myself and give my younger brother the smaller piece."

Before he cuts it, though, his father cautions him. "You may have received the right to cut the watermelon, but keep in mind that the right to choose the first piece is not reserved for you but for your brother." The older son immediately cuts the watermelon in two equal portions.

The father used out-of-the-box thinking in challenging his son in this manner. Of course, this same process can be adopted for larger matters as well.

Here is another excellent example of thinking out-of-the-box.

Two women of the same age were arguing over an empty seat on the bus. One of them said, "I saw the seat first." The other countered by claiming she had laid a handkerchief on the seat first so that she could sit on it.

The conductor noticed these two women arguing and made a suggestion. "Instead of arguing over who gets to sit there, solve it using the only logical means available. Discuss who, out of the two of you, is older. And then the older woman will sit on the seat." Hearing this, both the women abandoned the seat and instead gave it to a woman who was older than them!

Thus, the out-of-the-box thinking of the conductor easily put an end to the quarrel.

Out-of-the-box thinking makes you "new." When you apply a new effort or approach a problem from a new perspective, then you have effectively changed it. When you apply a creative approach to problem solving, the entire process of doing work changes. When you develop this habit, you'll notice first and foremost that you enjoy the work "in the moment" more. You'll also discover, though, that you've assimilated a habit that will work wonders in your life.

Each individual has his own set of thought patterns, which usually holds him a prisoner. He is unable to think out of that pattern. That's why it's so crucial that you break free of this old structure of thinking and get into the habit of thinking in new and innovative ways.

When you do this, you save more time than you can ever imagine—time that you previously wasted thinking "in the old ways." It won't happen overnight, but if you're patient and give it a little time, you'll be pleasantly surprised at how much time you'll be saving. You'll also be amazed at this new thinking. Don't worry that you're not up for the task, because you are.

You see, out-of-the-box thinking doesn't necessitate that you completely overhaul your thoughts and find radically new ways of doing things. It merely means that you adopt the habit of thinking in a new way at least for some time, free from the old patterns of thought.

When you take this initial step, new insights will open up. Insights that you never noticed before or could never have imagined before. Start today. Begin working immediately on thoughts that save you time.

You must begin your out-of-the-box thinking, not only for your own personal benefit, but also for others associated with you—at home or at work. Don't get bogged down by the fact that at the moment you're not able to think this way. If you keep trying, keep applying new ideas, you discover one day that you've got it.

Thinking in this manner takes time. You can compare it to exercise. You don't buy new running shoes one day and run a marathon in them the next. No, you have to develop your muscles before you can run. In much the same way, you'll have to flex your thinking and develop a creative mindset before you discover this creative approach to work and life.

Out-of-the-box thinking releases the energy needed that brings things to completion. This energy brings full potentiality to whatever it touches. This energy brings forth all conceivable expansiveness of the object in question in its entirety.

Everything around us and even within us is constantly evolving. Everything is pregnant with possibilities. Anything which has not yet revealed its hidden potentialities, anything with its possibilities lying undiscovered, untapped, is then "incomplete" or not "new." Whatever is incomplete can only be made complete by the addition of something to it or by removing something unnecessary from it.

Out-of-the-box thinking is an art, the key that opens you up into limitless potential. It's the means by which you bring the "new" into your life. This "new" will enable you to break out of your programmed repetitive way of living. This "new" will welcome originality, innovation, and higher awareness into your life.

> *It has been my observation that most people get ahead during the time that others waste.*
>
> – Henry Ford

SAY "NO" AND SAVE YOUR TIME

Give importance to your time

*Learn to say "no" to everything that takes you away
from the attainment of your life purpose.*

How many times has this happened to you? Somebody asks you to take on a project or a task. It could be anything from taking part in a play to tackling writing a white paper for someone. Before you even have the chance to think about it, you hear yourself saying "yes."

"Where did that come from?" you ask within. But the damage is done. You're committed to a project. Just what you need. Another task to place on your list. The sad part is that you have no one to blame but yourself.

It's bad enough you have any number of tasks on your list that are not complete and now you have added yet another one.

So, why did you say yes? If you're like many other individuals, you agreed because you simply couldn't say no. Did you know, however, that if you would have said "no" to that and similar unnecessary tasks, you could save much time and energy?

When you say yes to these tasks, you do nothing more than "shoot yourself in the foot." Let's say a friend asks you to do something and refuses to take no for an answer. Every time you try to decline, he puts increasing pressure on you. Against your better judgment, you finally relent. Now you're strapped with another task and need to make time to do so. What's worse, you have no absolutely no enthusiasm for that activity.

Before you agree to take an "unimportant" project on, listen to your conscience. Ask yourself, whose responsibility is this project? Does it fall under your responsibility? If it isn't part of your important tasks and, instead, belongs to another individual, then you are under no obligation to agree to do it. In fact, you need to stand your ground and politely and gently say no to undertaking it.

What is the best way to say no?

How do you refuse to assume another task for which you really don't have the time, energy, or enthusiasm? The best way is simply to communicate this directly to the said person. When you don't want to do a task, don't say "I can't do this." Instead make it crystal clear and say, "I will not do this task."

Do you notice the subtle difference in these two refusals? At first glance, there may not seem like much of a difference, but after you study them for even a short time, you can discern the meaning of each one. Each sentence produces different results. The best way to explain this is through an illustration.

> There were two groups who were asked to do a specific job. The first group was told to refuse the job by saying, "We cannot do this job." The second group was instructed to refuse by saying, "We will not do this job."

When both groups were pressured to perform the task, the first group (the I-cannot-do-this-job group) spent 70 percent of their time on the task. This compares to the amount of time the second group spent: only 35 percent of their time. This is because the implications of both statements actualize in different ways.

When you tell someone "I can't do this task," it also has the meaning that you can do it, or you're capable of doing it, if the said person would continue to push you a bit further. When, on the other hand, you respond with the powerful statement, "I will not do this," that "will not" stands in there in determination and defiance. It does not allow for a bit of give or wiggle room.

Imagine a shopkeeper who tells you, "I cannot give you any discount on these clothes." You visit another shopkeeper who says, "I won't give you a discount on these clothes." If you had to choose from these two statements, which one embodies a resolve? You may wrangle and coax a yes out of the first shopkeeper. However, you may hesitate to try and bargain with the second one.

Keep this in mind the next time you need to turn down a job. Instead of saying "I cannot do this job," say instead, "I will not do this job." Once you try it, you'll discover that it's actually a very simple way to say "no."

Getting into the habit of saying no is possible. And it is a habit. But when you must turn down a job, do it as politely as you can, giving the individual requesting your help as much respect as possible. And above all, don't beat around the bush. If you have no intention of taking on the task, don't lead the other person on thinking you might do it. Be sure that the person understands that you certainly do respect him. Many times, individuals have refused a job and attempted to give the other person respect in the process. But the person being turned down was unable for whatever reason to understand that.

Ensure when you say no that it is not a reflection of the other person, but a reflection of your already large to-do list. Saying yes to a project you probably can't complete only gets you tangled up in your own web. If you were to take it on and not complete it, then your reliability diminishes. Intelligence is not in jumping out of the frying pan and into the fire. It means that by evading a bit of discomfort now—saying no—you'll only be inviting a bigger problem later on.

When you hesitate and try to escape from saying no and instead give in and say yes, you only invite trouble on yourself. You don't say no because you feel that person may be offended. If this is your reason for accepting the job, think about this for a few moments. That individual will only feel offended and upset for a few minutes when you turn him down. But if you say yes and then not complete the task, you have lost your trustworthiness and reliability. That is an expensive deal. By attempting to evade an unpleasant, uncomfortable moment, you now have to face the possibility of losing something even larger—that person's trust in you. You face the loss of your reputation.

So, remember if you're not planning on accepting the assignment, simply say, "I will not do this work; I don't have the time." Say this with respect, not with any harshness or arrogance. You can explain to them that "I would definitely want to do it, but due to other priorities I will not be able to do it, please forgive me." When you speak directly with respect, people do not feel so offended, as much as they would if you would say yes and not accomplish the task.

"What you say, you do"

If you do what you say, people are able to put their trust in you and you are considered reliable. Here's a good illustration of this lesson. Suppose, you tell your employee that if he doesn't perform well at work, he may lose his job. When faced with this, the employee immediately improves his performance. He knows you will do what you say. In essence, people trust your word.

In order to become trustworthy and reliable, you must develop two qualities. The first is courage. The second is being free from deception. Here, courage means having the fortitude to face the truth. Once you're able to communicate with others courageously and without adopting any dishonest methods, the trust people have placed on you will only grow exponentially.

People slowly begin to understand that the one who speaks directly and with respect does not deceive or cheat anyone. He or she is straightforward and is able to speak their mind clearly.

However, it cannot be overemphasized that while being straightforward, common sense should also be used.

For a while, you'll probably feel strange while cultivating this habit. You may hesitate, and even be a bit fearful in politely telling others you can't accept any more tasks. But, you'll also be developing your courage to say no and you'll feel good being free from participating in any deception. And rest assured when you do this, you'll certainly be reaping rewards in the future. This single habit can save you a lot of time, if you let it. So the quicker it becomes second nature to you, the better.

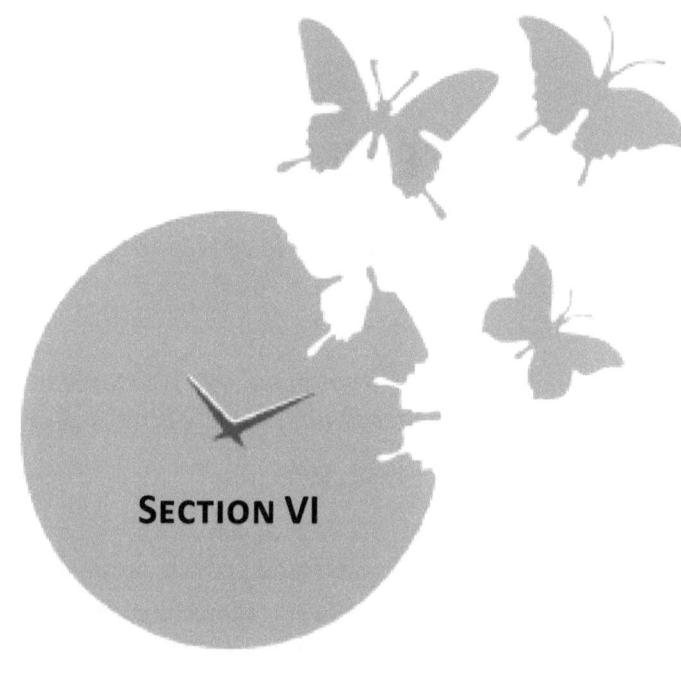

SECTION VI

RIGHT INVESTMENT OF THE WEALTH OF TIME

SAVE TIME AND INVEST IT

Fortify your investment planning

If something is worth doing, then put your heart and soul into it. Infuse your productivity with the power of present-mindedness.

Yes, you've already seen (and perhaps already implemented) that you can save much time using the techniques in this book. So, what plans do you have for the time you've so dutifully saved?

What? You haven't thought about it yet? There's no time like the present to begin to give this some thought. After all, you sure didn't go through all of that just to squander it away on watching mindless television, playing mobile games, or simply sleeping late.

Of course, part of the time you'll find yourself taking time out for all of these things. They do make nice celebratory gifts to yourself on occasion. But if you are frequently indulging in them, then all the effort you used in saving time has been wasted.

Now's the time to decide what productive steps you will take in investing time—before you develop bad habits with regard to handling your newfound time. You may think this a bit strange, but it's easier than you think for you (or anyone for that matter).

Think about the process of saving and investing. It's very clear that the money you save, you don't do so for the sole purpose of spending it foolishly and irresponsibly. In fact, mostly the complete opposite is true. You save money, for the most part, because you want to see it multiply even more in the future. The money you saved and then invested to multiply it makes you feel financially empowered.

You should receive the same feeling, the same empowerment, when you save time. The trouble with this is you can't see, count, and record the time you save as with money. You can't withdraw the time out of an account in the bank when you're running a bit short, like you can with money. Yes, time is intangible. You can't really see how much you have actually saved and you seldom, if ever, think about how you are going to invest the saved time.

Along the same lines, you may be tempted to take the money you have saved and spend a portion of it. That makes you feel good, but admit it, not for long. Then there's the fact that once you spend it, that money does not come back to you and neither does it grow for you. In the same way, when you spend your "hard earned time," you feel good for some time. But, you don't really get any returns or output, do you?

Before you invest time in any activity, you should always ask yourself, "Am I spending time or am I investing it, and how can I tell the difference?"

To decide this properly, you must determine if the time you're going to use will provide you with "returns" now or in the future, or is it just a momentary delight. Once you think about it, you'll receive the answer almost immediately.

A good example of this test is, suppose you decide you are going to watch a movie. But, it's a movie you've already seen before. You ask yourself, "Will I get any benefit out of these two hours I spend watching it beyond the two hours of enjoyment? Will watching this movie benefit me in any way in the future?"

As soon as you ask this question, you will understand if your time has been invested or just spent.

On the other hand, time spent in reading a good book is never wasted. When you read, you'll acquire knowledge on how to invest productively thousands of hours of your future.

Having this type of awareness of the value of time is important. Once you begin to pay attention and ask these questions, you'll find it's easier to decide how to utilize the time you've saved through the methods in this book. You've made great strides in saving time. Now, you need to invest it well.

A good example of spending and investing time can be seen every morning. Many individuals decide to wake up early. So they do. But then when they realize they haven't planned what they are going to do with this extra time, they may go back to sleep. So, if you can save 30 minutes through time management techniques, you must also deliberate what you will invest these 30 minutes in.

If you haven't planned anything better to do with your saved time, then you can use it to check all your present activities once more to ensure they are completed accurately. Or you could use this time to perform your present activity consciously and carefully.

Let's say that for saving time, you kicked off your shoes in a rush, threw your keys, and hurried to your room. But then you saw your bed and laid down. It would be so much better to have kept the shoes and keys in their proper places. At the very least, that ensures you're not wasting your time searching for them later.

In much the same way, think about when your visit a relative. Before you jump up to leave hastily, think about what's waiting at home that absolutely must get accomplished.

If there are no pressing tasks at home, then why don't you take this time and use it well visiting a bit longer. In this way, the present time is used in a satisfactory manner and to its fullest good.

Think about it. Any "free time" that you have can be used for sowing seeds for the future, allowing your qualities and talents to flourish. But you also need to approach this with the knowledge that far too often, many individuals fall into the trap of negative thinking during their spare time. That's why you need to deliberately focus on magnifying your qualities and skills, to avoid such thinking which can only bring negative results in your life.

In preparation for the time you've freed by following the suggestions in this guide, you may decide to make a list of relevant tasks you can do in your free time. In this way, you'll know where to invest this valuable time. You could create separate lists of activities you can do for work and for your household. Some individuals even make a list of things they can do while watching television. Below are some ideas for utilizing your spare time.

1. Manage your time

It's only after you manage your time will you be able to handle it properly. Perhaps you feel that much of your time is wasted executing some important activities. But this isn't so. In the future, this time will prove to be quite beneficial to you. Just as the time you've spent in school proves most useful throughout your lifetime.

Some individuals think that the time they spent in school would have been better used somewhere else. "My career or business would have reached greater heights. I would have earned more money."

While that may be how they feel, it's an incorrect assumption. The fifteen or so years invested in education provides direction to the seventy-five years that lie ahead of us. Yes, you may earn more money during that time. But the expertise and knowledge on such activities as how to account for or how to manage money can only be acquired by educating yourself. The money invested in a good education never goes to waste.

Let's say an uneducated man started earning a living five years prior to an educated one. The educated one during that five years had been going to school. Yet, the man who went to school and supposedly "wasted" his time can earn the same amount of money as the other gentleman, only in a shorter time period. Most importantly, though, is that the man with the education can also direct others onto the right path.

The same thing goes for time management. The individual who has invested time toward the planning and management of time is able to use his time well. Those individuals who don't learn how to manage their time, may waste it at various places. These individuals would do well if they were to take some time out for the planning and management of time.

2. Invest your time in reading (a good book, or your diary, or task list)

If you've written down a task list, then you can always reap the benefits of this in your free time. It's amazing what you have learned that has faded with time. When you read your list, it will jog your memory, keeping them fresh and rooted in your mind. When you read your task list, you'll be reminded of the next steps or activities you need to undertake to get those projects to progress toward completion.

Many successful individuals have the habit of reading books in their free time. They know that books are a great source of guidance on all topics. Besides that, it adds to your knowledge of language and vocabulary. Today, reading a book is easier than ever with the development of e-books, accessible not only on dedicated e-book readers but also on your laptop and mobile.

3. Sow seeds in your free time, learn something new

When people talk about learning something new, many say, "Let me learn something that will help me get a better job or a promotion." They don't think about learning just for the sake of taking in new knowledge. Far too many of them talk merely about learning new ideas and concepts related to their career. Why not begin to learn about a completely different subject? You can learn to dance, play an instrument, perform some art projects, or even learn first aid. Your range of interests may run the gamut from cooking to new languages to mind science.

When you first start off learning in this direction, you may wonder what could possibly be gained by this. But, if you continue along this route, then your ability to understand things increases. You will gain a new perspective on things around you. Additionally, you will develop a new skill and you will be able to think of creative solutions to apply in your field.

4. Associate yourself with service and help others

In your newly found free time, you may want to volunteer your services somewhere. It's said that only when you avail yourself to others to perform service-oriented activities that you'll be able to truly understand what measure of happiness and fulfilment service generates. There really is no better way of using your free time than in investing it in helping your fellow men and trying to bring a change.

Think for a moment or two how you would like to serve and whom you'd like to help. With this is mind, find out when you'll have the opportunity to do it. If you have a desire for social service and have a specific cause in mind, then you need to associate yourself with a group that works along those lines.

Believe it or not, through serving others, you'll develop wisdom, specialization, as well as a sense of honor. You will also find it to be an unbelievably fulfilling experience. Devoting your free time to a worthy cause will, without a doubt, create joy and contentment in your life.

5. Develop a hobby

Do you have a hobby? Did you have one when you were younger? Why not resurrect your old hobby or find a new one for your free time? Find an activity that aligns with the activities you enjoy. You can start by meeting people who share your interests. You can share your experiences in this area with them. And if you're going to re-ignite an old hobby or find a new one, look at it as a chance of attaining a new and exciting level of potential in that activity. Let's say, you're going to paint. You had done it years before, but haven't picked up a brush in a very long time. If you're going to paint, then don't limit yourself to acrylic or even to water colors.

Open yourself out and see what you can do in all areas of painting. You may even try your hand at sculpture.

If you don't have a specific hobby, why not invest time in your health? With this great investment, the time that's wasted in being ill can be saved. After all, if you don't exercise, the chances of you becoming ill grow. And if this should occur, you'll find yourself using a lot of your precious time in regaining your health.

6. Meditate

Contrary to what some individuals believe, meditation is one of the most important investments in the future you can make. Sure, there are those who watch others sit in silence and remark, "In this time they're devoting to doing nothing, they could have finished some important tasks." Others, however, understand just how valuable meditation is. The reality is that the amount of work that is done on the mind during meditation cannot be accomplished at any other time. Your mind is your most powerful tool. The sharper the tool, the more impressive your work and the better use of your time.

But don't save mediation only for your free time. Be sure to include it in your daily schedule. You'll be surprised at the pleasant changes that take place in all aspects of your life and also how much more you're able to complete in a day.

7. Organize things; get cleaning done

Are the spaces in which you live, work, even drive, free from clutter? If the answer is no, then you now have another alternative what you can do with your new free time. What about your mobile or your laptop? Are they cluttered with unused apps, old emails that need clearing out, and read texts that are no longer relevant?

Decide when you have the free time and then you can align it with what needs to be organized and cleaned. If you only have five minutes before a meeting, for example, then you might know that you can at least clear out unwanted emails and posts from your mobile and laptop in that time period. Got a bit more time? Then you may use it to clear your desk drawer or put your files in order. Some people are careless with regards to cleanliness. However, a clean and tidy house and environment is liked by all. So, whenever you get the time, you can start cleaning. Don't wait for Diwali or other festivals to do it.

8. Meet and spend time with friends or relatives

This is always a wonderful way to use your free time. Today, with the mobile, it's easier than ever to have the phone numbers of friends and family at your fingertips. Why not speak with those you haven't connected with in a while? You could even resolve to call them once a month to catch up with what they're doing. Meet up with a few people, especially those you care about and those that care about you. This helps maintain warmth in your relationships.

If you do not want to give much time to socializing, still take out a little time for it so that you can live within the society in harmony. By being connected with people, you can share your ideas with them, and in doing so, your mind will expand as will your experiences and perspective on life.

Don't think that because it's called "free time," it's less important than your scheduled time. You'll be amazed at how you reap the fruits of the seeds that you sow in your free time throughout your life.

GET HI-TECH

Become a master of new technology and new thinking

> *If something can be done tomorrow
> but not today as you wanted,
> it's not the end of the world.*

If you had your choice, which tool would you use for a specific purpose? Would you use the one that appears to be a perfect fit or the instrument that's outdated?

Of course, you'd use the perfect fit. All things being equal, it would probably save you time, energy, and much frustration.

In a similar vein, the person who has proven himself to be a skilled learner and to put new techniques into practice will probably be the individual who receives the promotion—any promotion, regardless of what industry they work in. Those who are rigid in their thinking and continue to cling to the old, trite, and often outdated modes of accomplishing work normally will not be even considered for a better position.

If you want to receive a promotion or at least remain an effective

SIX

and relevant member of your corporation, you need to accept the changes that have occurred with time in the ways of working and adapt to them. You also have to be vigilant and keenly aware of new technology and become tech-savvy. In effect, you must not only be a practitioner of these newest methods, but an agile and quick learner. When a change of technology occurs that could help you perform your duties better and faster, you can check it out and decide if it could make a difference for the better.

How do you accomplish this? If no other way, then through the tried and true "trial and error" method. This process is rather simple. What is the new item you wish to learn? Research on it and begin to use it, according to your understanding of the item at the moment.

After you start using the tool the first time, stop for a minute or so. Scrutinize what you have achieved and then think about the ways you can improve your performance with it. What are the various ways you could use it? Then, keep using it. As you use it, you'll become more skilled and increase your speed as well as your overall knowledge of the tool. Soon, you'll feel competent in using it. And before you know it, your colleagues may even come to you to learn how to use it, considering you to be the expert.

Your ability to achieve any goals—career, professional, or home life—increases when you have visualized in your mind the task being performed from the beginning to end. This means that if you want to become skilled at any task, first see yourself performing it flawlessly.

How can you use this in regard to the new technology you've embraced? Simple. While learning to use a computer, for example, imagine yourself pressing the necessary buttons, turning on the monitor successfully, logging into the machine, and working on the software that you need to learn. Do this and you'll see how much more quickly you will be using it with a minimum of hassle and frustration. You could easily invest a portion of your holiday or free time in this way.

Additionally, appreciate those moments you are alone as valuable. Then use this time for self-development as well as to make new discoveries towards being hi-tech.

Becoming hi-tech means you are able to operate up-to-date technology, like e-mail, electronic tablets and laptops, as well as the newest applications on the mobile. There's no doubt about it, science has showered us with many conveniences through technology.

We all have to learn how to use modern technology, there's no getting around it. This is especially true if your career uses it in any form. But more than that, everyone in this modern era must learn how to use it in the proper way if you want to be fully trained for your best self-expression.

Don't let doubt enter your mind. You cannot waiver on whether you are capable of learning. You can't ask yourself, "How can I learn this, when I have never even touched a computer till date?" If your goal is to plan and manage time efficiently, you must become proficient at new technology, you must become hi-tech.

If you don't think you are capable of learning how to use even the basics of a computer, consider this. There are many individuals who don't know a thing about operating a computer, but once they are assigned work that requires using one, they learn. During the training, they encounter many challenges, they need to ask the same questions over and over again because they forget one thing or another. "Which key is for what function, again?" "Where did I save that file in the computer? I can't find it anywhere."

But despite all this, they keep trying, they continue to practice, and soon they know how to operate a computer.

The bottom line is simply this: you can learn any task. Alas, though, there is one caveat. You must be eager to learn from the very core of your heart. Then start learning as soon as possible basic things like sending text messages on the mobile, sending emails, or accessing or researching information on the computer. You should know how every information can be sent everywhere sitting on a computer or using your cell phone.

You have no doubt heard the adage: "Time is money." This means that when you can do something faster and more proficiently, then you're saving money. It's only logical then that you should work to use the full range of benefits your laptop, mobile, or any other piece of technology offers for that matter. Today, you'll discover that it's not at all difficult to download a myriad of applications through the internet and find yourself being hi-tech. More individuals than ever before are planning and managing their time in advanced ways using technology. This saves them time as well as helps them to communicate with people on time.

The following illustration is a great example of how saving time can indeed save money.

> The manager of a company posted information about his firm on Wikipedia. His goal was to reach all of his employees so they knew the basics of how the firm operated. By using this technology, he saved time while connecting with his employees. Not only this, now the public at large

also learned about the direction and purpose of the firm.

But wait, there was still another layer of benefit to using technology in this manner. The manager noticed that since everyone had the same access to the same information, they were effortlessly and smoothly able to make decisions related to their work. They were, in effect, pressing onward together in the same direction with a common goal.

It's by participating in the hi-tech evolution that you'll be able to discover new and exciting solutions that previously stumped you.

Below, read about an employee who went hi-tech and why.

> "When I realized that for my daily jobs, meetings, and for organizing my time, I must use the Outlook software, then I promptly began using it. Before that, I would use my diary in which I noted: when what job needs to be accomplished, and when to meet whom, and other entries. I had never operated a software like Outlook before. But when I began using it, I found that I saved almost 50% of my time when I wrote the description of the work and meetings in the Outlook instead of in the diary. I utilized the time I saved by investing it into new plans, like meeting the company's customers once a month and contacting new prospective clients, and my success grew exponentially."

If you feel that you are unable to achieve success in a particular job or activity, then your next step should be to change the process by which you are carrying out your job. When you take a familiar task and do it in a novel way, you'll find new dimensions and new facets in the task. And the bonus is that you'll be saving time in the process.

MAKE DECISIONS AT THE RIGHT TIME

Learn this art through an easy technique

*50% of your time must be intricately planned.
25% of your time, you must work with your instinctive or intuitive mind
—it's fine if you can or cannot complete all your tasks.
25% of your time must be left alone; it will seek its work on its own.*

Have you noticed the one trait that all people who find success in life have in common? They all make decisions at the right time. Hence, the decision to invest your time in cultivating this habit is an excellent one.

While history forgives those who have made wrong decisions, it seems there is no forgiveness for those who don't take any decision at all. If you decide that you don't want to make a decision, then this decision too must be taken after thinking on it. That's because there are consequences of not taking decisions too.

Far too many individuals find it difficult to make decisions. There's an easy process that can help you break free of the inability to make decisions. It's simply this: Notice the options or alternatives to the problem that are available to you. Then start making small "bite-sized" decisions.

Don't worry if one of these small decisions ends up being wrong. The important aspect of this part of the process is the fact that you made a decision. The more you approach problems and situations in this manner, the more right decisions you'll be making after a while. And in the meantime, these small decisions won't have monumental consequences tied to them.

It appears that many individuals are not generally good at making decisions. Why? That's because most of your truly important decisions from the time you were young to adulthood were made by others around you. You didn't choose your name. Your parents did. Your schooling—especially at the earliest levels—was also a choice made by others. And if you think about it, in many families even the choice of what college to go to are made by other family members, as well as where they will work, right up to the decision of who they will marry. In those families in which the father is a strict disciplinarian by nature, the children are not allowed to make a decision for themselves until relatively later in life. It only seems natural, then, that when we need to make a big decision, we search for someone who can make the choice for us or at least tell us what's the right decision.

So, it seems that throughout your life, you have depended on others to make decisions for you. This is why your ability and capacity to decide for yourself weakens and diminishes with time. If you don't continually use your decision-making powers (and you know you have them), you begin to notice they atrophy, like any muscle not being used. If, by chance, you haven't made your own decisions in a while, there's no reason to think you cannot revive, renew, and reinvigorate this power. It just requires some cultivation on your part.

Good decisions come with experience and experience is gained by making decisions. Don't worry that some of your decisions might be wrong. You will gain experience from those too. Therefore, it's vital that you must begin to decide for yourself—and when you start with those small "bite-sized" choices, there's less fear associated with making a mistake. If you never make a bad or wrong decision, then you will never learn how to make right decisions.

In some homes, housewives seem to have far less ability to decide things for themselves. That's not to say they are not capable of doing so. But, if throughout the marriage, they have deferred to their husbands or other family members to even answer questions as simple as "What should I cook today?", they find themselves seeking answers for every choice they need to make.

In the long run, these persons end up encountering even more problems. But you can avoid this situation by using the technique provided below. Then you can start exercising those decision-making muscles.

> It's been shown that your mind loses more than 20 percent of energy in the process of thinking. That's why so many individuals limit the number and importance of the decisions they make in a single day. Did you know that the former U.S. President Barack Obama typically wears only blue or grey suits? He doesn't want to waste energy on such matters. He was quoted as saying, "I don't want to

make decisions about what I'm eating or wearing. Because I have too many other decisions to make."

Similarly, Obama used only one system when responding to memos. First, he gave more importance to written decisions than to verbal ones. When his advisors needed him to decide on an issue, they wrote a memo outlining what needs to be done. Once he read it, he would answer it using the three checkboxes at the bottom.

- ☐ Agree
- ☐ Disagree
- ☐ Let's discuss

In this way, the decision-making process not only became simpler but also less time-consuming.

When you have already decided on the "small bites" of choices, like what you're going to wear and eat as well as how you're going to approach your daily tasks, then you will find that you have more free time for other important tasks.

"Plus-minus-interesting" technique

While the suggestions explained previously are both effective and easy-to-use, the "plus-minus-interesting" technique is by far the simplest and most effective one in the endeavor for perfecting your decision-making capacity.

Often simply referred to as "P.M.I." it was first proposed by Edward de Bono, the father of lateral thinking and a brain-training pioneer.

When you make a decision, you'll find that some individuals will agree with you, while others won't. Those who agree with you are normally only able to see the positive angle of the decision. Those who disagree are more likely to view the negative aspects of your choice.

However, very often, you are actually "fenced in" within the boundaries of your own understanding of the problem as well as the reason you made the choice. So, once you say "yes" to a task, later saying "no" to it becomes difficult. Similarly, when you say "no" to a project, you will find you aren't able to say "yes" for it later on.

When you get a new concept or idea about a task you are performing, you're often so fascinated by the idea that you are unable to listen to anyone who gives you a negative assessment of the concept. This is the perfect situation to use the P.M.I. technique. You can use it to help you make a decision on anything, by the way.

When you use this technique, you need to focus on three aspects of the decision you're about to make:

1. **Plus points: Reflect upon the positive aspects**

List what you see as all of the positive aspects of the task. While you're doing this, sweep all the negativity out of your mind. Don't pay attention to any negative concerns at this point.

2. **Minus points: Ponder the negative aspects**

At this time, you need to write down all the negative points, flaws, and everything that could go wrong in the situation.

3. Interesting points: Consider the interesting facts

When you begin to think about the decision that you must make, you'll discover that there are indeed some factors that are neither positive nor negative. However, they are interesting or give a different perspective on things. These ideas or comments should be noted on the "Interesting" list.

When you analyze these three aspects of the project separately and find the solutions to the negative aspects, the process becomes simple and logical. The degree of how wrong or how correct a decision is cannot merely be based on an emotional process. Instead, any solid choice is based on understanding of the concept.

If that sounds less than simple and even a bit frightening, you're about to be pleasantly surprised. The truth of the matter is anyone can develop the talent for making sound decisions by following the P.M.I. method. Take hold of this technique as your own and you'll develop the habit of making right decisions at the right time. This means that going forward from here you are saving time and becoming time-wealthy.

Don't spend a dollar's worth of time on a ten-cent decision.

— Peter Turla

Smart Tip to Manage your Time

COMBINE EXERCISE AND WORK

Do you spend a lot of time in meetings with your employees?

If you do, then here's an easy way to get your exercise in and still maintain your productivity. You're well aware that just about all meetings take place around a desk or conference table in an office. If you are sincere about saving time—and grabbing a few minutes of exercise in the process—then conduct a walking meeting.

There are two benefits to this concept. The first is that those who are walking will talk only on the issue at hand. The second is that, of course, you're meeting some of your exercise requirements.

And there is a third, lesser known, benefit to a meeting like this. Many individuals find that walking stimulates their imagination and they can think up better concepts or methods of performing the tasks they are being charged with.

UTILIZE THE SMALL AMOUNTS OF TIME

Big use of bits of free time

*Time is a seed
which when sown consciously,
yields the fruit of success.*

You're probably wondering how we could even be talking about "free time," when there is a shortage of time in the first place. Perhaps you've heard the proverb: "A penny saved is a penny earned."

The same principle can be applied to time. It's really quite simple. Saving time gives you more time. If, for example, you have saved 10 rupees on every 100 rupees, that's 10 percent, then those 10 rupees are your earnings.

In much the same way, if a student has 100 days until his exams, he can think, "I have 90 days left." In this way, he can save 10 days—or 10 percent—and complete his studies in 90 days instead of 100. He can then use the remaining 10 days creatively. During this time, he can think of investing those days into studying areas that others would not think about since they don't have time.

He, in effect, has a 10-day advantage over the other students who slog until the day of the exams. This is the perfect time for the student who has saved his time to shine. This is what will lead to his growth and progress.

Be ready for free time

When you go to meet someone, more often than not you have to wait for some time for that person. In much the same way, when you leave home to handle something, you may find yourself waiting for one thing or another. All of us have resigned ourselves that waiting, regardless of what it's for, has become a regular part of our daily routine.

This is true whether you have an appointment with someone, are picking up the children from school, or even standing in a queue in front of a store cashier or a ticket window. How do you react to this time? Why not use these bits of time creatively? The next time you learn your flight is delayed or your doctor won't be available for another hour, don't get upset over it. Instead, consider this time as your free time—and view it as nothing less than a gift.

While going out, you can take your smart phone, a notepad, small books, etc. for good use of your free time. When you are "stuck" waiting, you can also use this time for contemplation on a subject which is important to you. Or you could reflect on your new ideas or thoughts that you would like to apply in your life. Author Jason Womack advises that if you carry some work with you everywhere, you will definitely find the time to complete it. It could be something as simple as replying to an e-mail, returning an important phone call, reviewing a proposal or preparing a new one, or even studying.

Every successful individual is not only aware of time but has respect for it. These persons know just how potent time is and only by the perfect use of it can they be and remain successful. Often, there's a long commute between your home and office. Salespersons, for example, spend most of their time travelling as a matter of fact. What you need to understand is that if you spend two-and-a-half hours commuting, then you spend about 10 percent of your life travelling.

While travelling, many people "spend" their time listening to music on their mobile, reading the newspaper, or even engaging in idle gossip. What they don't seem to realize is that if they read a motivational book during this time instead, listen to educational audios/videos, or engage in some vital tasks, they would be able to achieve their goals more quickly.

> When Napoleon Bonaparte, for example, went to war with his army, he used his travelling time or any other free time to write letters. Edison is famous that even as a teenager, he used his travelling time to working on his experiments. Bill Gates invested in his travel time by making important telephone conversations. In order to learn African geography, Gates at one time had posted a map of Africa in his garage. In this way, while he parked his car, turned off the ignition, and exited it, he was still using his time in a vital way—even though it was only a few moments.

Many individuals equate the weekend with entertainment. You may be surprised to learn that by getting some work completed on the weekends, you can actually lighten your burden of work throughout the following week. If every week, you made the commitment to use 2-3 hours of free time on the weekend to accomplish a few tasks, you'll notice that you still have plenty of time available for other activities.

No one likes to wait. But waiting, as we said before, seems to be an unavoidable part of life. If you're not waiting for a train, or a bus, or a cab, you're waiting for another person. To be truly successful and save time, you should have a list of small tasks to work on while you wait. If you have a list in your purse or pocket, then you won't have to suffer the restlessness of waiting. Instead, you'll end up feeling rather good about yourself having accomplished something in that time.

> *Don't say you don't have enough time.*
> *You have exactly the same number of hours per day*
> *that were given to Helen Keller, Pasteur,*
> *Michelangelo, Mother Teresa, Leonardo da Vinci,*
> *Thomas Jefferson, and Albert Einstein."*
>
> – H. Jackson Brown Jr.

TIME TO MEDITATE IN SOLITUDE

The spiritual technique of time management

*Work and rest with awareness:
Rest before you tire and start working before you feel lethargic.
In this way, your batteries are always charged.
Work can be accomplished with sustained momentum and
time can be saved.*

You can find many time-saving techniques in this book as you can in other books on this topic. If there's just one habit you can take away from this book, then, without a doubt, it should be that of making time in your schedule for solitude and silence.

It's during this time, when individuals sit alone in silence, that the great inventions and innovations of the world have been conceived. We are aware that some scientists got their greatest ideas when they were in a relaxed state of mind or just soaking in their bathtub!

If you don't practice silence in solitude, then you may not believe this. But once you decide to give yourself this amazing gift, you will find miracles happening. This is one of the very important reasons why you should never belittle any period of time that has been saved. When you begin to save time, then you'll discover for yourself the secret that's hidden within it.

What does solitary time in silence mean?

To achieve the ultimate goal of finding the magic in time saved, you must understand what "solitary time in silence" truly entails. It means taking 10-30 minutes out of your day—every day—to sit in complete silence and basically "do nothing." This is your time to be with yourself in solitude. When you get into this habit, you'll be able to achieve a glorious harmony between yourself and your day—a habit that can help you for a lifetime.

This wonderful addition to your day consists of two dimensions: solitude and silence. First, let us understand the idea of solitude. It isn't the same thing as being lonely. Loneliness can be equated with a feeling of an internal emptiness. Solitude, on the other hand, means internal fullness. In solitude, you are with yourself and apart from the world and everything related to worldly matters.

The second dimension of this concept is "silence." This means, as you might guess, silence, but not necessarily the type found in meditation. Instead, we're talking about *being* with yourself and thinking about your life in peace. Let us understand more about it.

How to use your solitary time in silence

Below are four important steps by which you can begin your tranquil silent time.

Time and place:

Find a specific place where you can spend your silent and peace-filled time. Most of the times, it could be a room in your home. It really doesn't matter where it is, as long as it is free of interruptions and you can feel comfortable there.

Then you dedicate a time when you stop doing whatever activities or assignments you had been doing. You can begin with as little as 10-15 minutes. The important part of this step is "continuity" or consistency. Considering this, it's better to start with just a small amount of time rather than a large, unrealistic chunk of time. You can always increase the time you sit in solitude as you go along.

Most individuals prefer to sit in silence first thing in the morning, when you're less likely to get interrupted or be bothered by excessive noise. But if there's another time of the day you believe would work better for you, then by all means, give it a try.

Relax:

Begin your time of solitude and silence with something relaxing, like sitting in meditation for some time, or spending some time in prayer, or even listening to music. You can do whatever relaxes you. Also, there is no need to sit in a particular posture. Just sit in a seat and get yourself comfortable. Being comfortable and relaxed is important. Don't stand or walk or run. If you want, you can focus on your breathing. But remember, relaxation is a step in this process, not the goal.

Don't do anything and also don't try 'not to do' anything:

After you have relaxed a few minutes, simply sit and do nothing. Our society is so used to being busy that many individuals may try to do "something" in this period which one has carved the time out to do nothing. You shouldn't even repeat a mantra or go into a formal meditative state. You have to do nothing. At the most, you can intermittently remind yourself, "I won't do anything, and also won't try 'not to do' anything."

Your silent time in solitude must be spent largely in this fashion. Yes, this is the most difficult step. But it's by going through this process that you will achieve the result. This, by the way, is also the step which lays the groundwork for the last step.

Think:

During your last five minutes in this session, think on any one area of your life. Contemplate peacefully. Take guidance from the source or the sacred space within you. You can think about any hobbies you have, about your passion, and even your habits. You can also reflect on how you spend your time. Or you can contemplate your spiritual life at this time as well. Take just one aspect of your life every day and think over it. You can also think about your schedule for the day.

After you've satisfied yourself thinking on one topic, then you can turn your mind briefly to those projects and activities you want to complete. In many ways, this is like mental time management. But, this small portion of time really does far greater things in your life than time management. Because, during this time, you are seeing the accomplishment of your most important activities for the day.

You're now in the perfect position to watch new thoughts and ideas arising within you. But don't just watch them. Capture them by writing them down on a piece of paper.

You can continue with this step for as much time as easily possible for you.

Why is it important to give time to solitary silence?

There are several primary reasons due to which sitting in solitary silence is vital to your overall well-being as well as your time management skills.

1. Relieves stress

It's no secret that we live in a stressful society. There's extreme stress as well as stress-related illnesses all around us. You can help alleviate it in your life and find a source of peace simply by making the time to spend by yourself. After it becomes a habit, you'll be surprised at how refreshed these few minutes, consistently executed, can make you feel. Once you feel refreshed, then you're ready to step into the world again and face the challenges and problems the day throws at you.

2. Helps you solve problems

Just by sitting and contemplating the problem, thinking about how it arose, thinking about the best way to solve it… this can help you find good solutions to your problem.

Even if you can't arrive at a solution to the problem, you have nevertheless, meditated on it. You'll discover that this only increases your resolve to discover an answer. And when you do this, your courage to progress grows, and you are rewarded with a deep internal peace.

3. Helps you understand yourself better

One of the best benefits to come out of this solitary time, though, is that you come to understand yourself better. After all, do you really know yourself? Do you think you know who you truly are? Surprisingly, most people don't. By spending time with yourself, you may not be able to get the complete answer to this question, but you'll definitely become aware how your life is going on and how you feel about it. You'll be better able to understand who you are and how you fit into this world.

4. Increases your tolerance and peace of mind

Do you feel that you are quite irritated as you experience shortage of time? Do you easily get angry with people? The more you think of people as annoying or difficult, the more you'll discover exactly that—more individuals who are annoying or difficult to deal with. *You cannot change the world; you cannot stop people from saying things.* So, stop trying. You can only change one thing. That one thing is your own perception, your own point of view. Once you have spent some time alone with yourself in silence, you'll find that you feel less irritated and less sad. Not only that, you will discover that you are in a far more peaceful state than before you started this process. The benefits don't end there. As you make this solitude time a daily activity, you'll discover that you have, within yourself, increased capacity for tolerance.

5. Increases productivity

By spending time with yourself, you're spending some time thinking about your work and how to manage your time. In the last step, you focused your thoughts on a portion of your life. You can also think about your daily duties and tasks: what goal would you want to achieve today? What step do you need to take today in order to eventually complete the goal? By pondering peacefully on these aspects, you can effectively increase your productivity.

The only fact to remember about these points is that you need to consistently and repeatedly perform this exercise. With just a few minutes a day, practiced every day of the week, you'll not only notice how the silence is helping you personally, but also in managing your time in the best manner, as well as in practicing and perfecting the techniques discussed in this book.

> *How many days are there in a year?*
> *Don't be fooled by the calendar.*
> *There are only as many days in the year as you make use of.*
> *One man gets only a week's value out of a year*
> *while another man gets a full year's value out of a week.*
>
> *– Charles Richards*

Bonus Chapter

BELIEFS ABOUT TIME

"I don't have time." Is this a belief? A belief is something which people believe in but which is actually not the truth; it's just their imagination. There are so many beliefs embedded in every individual's mind and they function according to those beliefs.

There was a logical reason behind the formation of every belief in the ancient times. But now the reasons have been lost, while the beliefs have remained. For example, one of the beliefs is that one should not sweep the house or throw away rubbish at night. Electricity had not been discovered when this belief was formed, and there was always a possibility that something valuable may be swept away in the darkness. But now there is no point to this belief due to presence of bright electric lights.

So, there are a number of minor as well as major beliefs operating in your life. And what's interesting is that you may or may not be fully aware that you have those beliefs. Some of them may not affect you much, but some of them may be severely restricting as well as harmful for your growth and progress. We should find the courage to discover the truth behind these beliefs and attain freedom from them.

There are many beliefs regarding time management too in our minds. It's essential to bring them to light and know their truth. Let us come face-to-face with some of the beliefs related to time and their reality.

Belief 1: We can control time and preserve saved time.

Reality: We can do neither. If we try to control time, our efforts would prove futile because by the end of the day, time escapes us just like sand from our fingers. We get only 24 hours every day. Now the only key in our hands is how we use this time available to us. If we want, we can use it wisely or we can totally waste it. But we cannot save and keep time with us like money. It is lost at the end of the day.

Belief 2: Time management means the art of performing maximum work in minimum time.

Reality: That's what some people believe about time management but it's not true. The real meaning of time management is accomplishing the most important tasks in the available time. We may possibly not be able to finish all the work that we would want to. Hence, if we can prioritize our tasks and focus on completing the most important ones, we can achieve our goals more effectively.

Belief 3: Phone calls, uninvited guests, and meetings are the main causes of wasting time.

Reality: This is a myth. The reality is all these activities are essential at times and not just a waste of time. The main cause of wasting time is wrong habits. Such as the tendency of procrastination, remaining entangled in thoughts of work, misplacing things and then searching for them, getting stuck in a task and being unable to move forward due to the insistence of perfection, continuing to carry on useless activities, and so on. These examples can make us realize that our wrong habits are our biggest enemies. The basic mantra for success is not to blame others but to discipline ourself.

Belief 4: We should not take on another task when we already have one. We should try to finish it first and then move on to another. This is the most effective way of working.

Reality: This undoubtedly seems to be an effective method of working but is not very effective when you actually start working in that manner. That's because very rarely you get a long chunk of time in which you can finish something in one sitting. It has been observed that it works more effectively if you divide your projects into small parts and work on them every day for some time. Decide the priority of all those tasks and then go for a 100-meter dash daily rather than attempting a marathon at one go.

Belief 5: We should create separate planners for office and home.

Reality: Totally opposite to this belief, you should prepare a single planner because it's you who has to be involved in all the activities on the planner. You have to give time to work and people, be it at school, home, office, market, and so forth. You should schedule all your professional as well as personal activities in one planner. The advantage is that then your professional activities won't adversely affect your personal activities or family time.

Belief 6: I alone can do this work faster and better. Nobody else will be able to do it. It would be just a waste of time.

Reality: People who want every task to be done perfectly and punctually are the ones who believe that only they can do so, and therefore insist on doing everything on their own. They are unable to tolerate a single flaw, which in the long run proves to be an expensive deal indeed. They should relinquish the need to do everything themselves and delegate some activities to others. This is like a good investment and after some time you will start reaping its benefits. The biggest benefit is that you will find that the work you allotted has been accomplished efficiently and successfully, and you also got the time to do something more important.

Belief 7: I should meet everyone's expectations and please everyone by doing everything they ask me to.

Reality: It's not necessary that every person's work and expectations would match with your priorities and lifestyle. Sometimes people's expectations are untimely and unsuitable, which may be impossible for you to fulfill. You may have to change yourself or your workstyle to satisfy those people. Hence, before taking on a new responsibility, think in detail about what are your requirements and duties, and only after that go on to help others.

Belief 8: Just making a to-do list is time management.

Reality: Simply making a list of all the tasks you need to do is not time management. Your feelings, priorities, and your attitude towards your work play a pivotal role in your time management. Because this is what inspires you to work. If you are not inspired to work, it has a deep impact on your tasks. Therefore, it's important to synchronize all these factors while making your to-do list.

Belief 9: You may plan your time in detail, but some unexpected tasks always pop up, which ruins your time-table. So, what's the point of time management?

Reality: The significance of time management does not diminish due to the above reason. If you plan in a proper manner, then you can handle even the sudden and unexpected tasks. You can do so by allotting some time in your time-table for unexpected activities, and then deciding when you will complete the work that was left unfinished due to the unexpected tasks. You can also use this new information for your work. Additionally, you should improve and strengthen your communication with the concerned people, so that the problem of sudden assignments popping up can be tackled at the root.

Belief 10: I can complete all my tasks with hard work.

Reality: *The more you work hard, the more you will achieve.* Is this a belief that has been passed on since the olden days? The fact is only hard work is not the key to success. Working with a judicious plan and completing it in a short time is the key.

Belief 11: I don't even have the time for time management, then why should I waste my time on it?

Reality: If you don't have time for time management, it indicates that you need time management all the more. This is because with time management you realize that you *can* complete all your important tasks along with saving time for something else.

The principle of time management says: An hour invested in preparing an accurate planner can save you 3-4 hours in the execution of that plan. It's a harmful habit to jump into an important activity without a plan.

You may have noted your beliefs related to time management from the ones mentioned above, and hopefully you would be working on getting rid of those myths. Very often, we continue to operate our lives believing our notions to be true. We don't challenge or try to break them. When these beliefs come to light and we discover the reality, that's when the possibility of breaking those beliefs increases. The next time any belief related to time management appears before you, become aware and ignore it. Then move ahead to take charge of your time.

A year from now, you may wish you had started today.

– Karen Lamb

You can send your opinion or feedback on this book to :

Tejgyan Foundation, Pimpri Colony, P. O. Box 25,
Pimpri, Pune – 411017 (Maharashtra), INDIA.
email : mail@tejgyan.com

Tejgyan... The Road Ahead
What is Tejgyan?

Tejgyan is the wisdom of the existential truth, which is beyond duality. "Gyan" is a term commonly used for "knowledge". Tejgyan is the wisdom beyond knowledge and ignorance. It is understanding that arises from direct experience of the final truth. It is what sets us free from the limitations of the mind and opens us to our highest potential.

In today's world, there are people who feel disharmony and are desperately trying to achieve balance in an unpredictable life. Tejgyan helps them in harmonizing with their true nature, the Self, thereby restoring balance in all aspects of their lives.

And then, there are those who are successful, but feel a sense of emptiness within. Tejgyan provides them fulfilment and helps them to embark on a journey towards self-realization. There are others who feel lost and are seeking the meaning of life. Tejgyan helps them to realize the true purpose of human life.

All this is possible with Tejgyan due to a very simple reason. The experience of the ultimate truth (God or Pure consciousness) is always available. The direct experience of this truth is possible provided the right method is known. Tejgyan is that method, that understanding.

The understanding of Tejgyan makes it possible to lead a life of freedom from fear, worry, anger and stress. It helps in attaining physical vitality, emotional strength and stability, harmony in relationships, financial freedom and spiritual progress.

At Tej Gyan Foundation, Sirshree imparts this understanding through a System for Wisdom – a series of retreats that guides participants step by step towards realizing the true Self, being established in the experience of self-realization, and expressing its qualities. This system for wisdom has been accredited with the ISO 9001:2015 certification.

Maha Aasmani Param Gyan Shivir

"**Maha Aasmani Param Gyan Shivir**" is the flagship Self-realization retreat offered by Tej Gyan Foundation. The retreat is conducted in Hindi. The teachings of the retreat are non-denominational (secular).

This residential retreat is held for 3 to 5 days at the foundation's MaNaN Ashram amidst the glory of the mountains and the pristine beauty of nature. The Ashram is located at the outskirts of the city of Pune in India, and is well connected by air, road and rail. The retreat is also held at other centres of Tej Gyan Foundation across the world.

You can participate in this retreat to attain ageless wisdom through a unique System for Wisdom so that you can:

1. Discover "Who am I" through direct experience.
2. Learn to abide in pure consciousness while functioning in the world, allowing the qualities of consciousness like peace, love, joy, compassion, abundance and creativity to manifest.
3. Acquire simple tools to use in everyday life, which help quiet the chattering mind.
4. Get practical techniques to be in the present and connect to the source of all answers within (the inner guru).
5. Discover missing links in the practices of Meditation (Dhyana), Action (Karma), Wisdom (Gyana) and Devotion (Bhakti).
6. Understand the nature of your body-mind mechanism to attain freedom form its tendencies.
7. Learn practical methods to shift from mind-centered living to consciousness-centered living.

A Mini-retreat is also conducted, especially for teenagers (14 to 16 years of age) during summer and winter vacations.

To register for retreats, visit www.tejgyan.org, contact (+91) 9921008060, or email mail@tejgyan.com

About Tej Gyan Foundation

Tej Gyan Foundation (TGF) was established with the mission of creating a highly evolved society through all-round development of every individual that transforms all the facets of their lives. It is a non-profit organization, founded on the teachings of Sirshree.

The Foundation has received the ISO certification (ISO 9001:2015) for its system of imparting wisdom. It has centres all across India as well as in other countries. The motto of Tej Gyan Foundation is 'Happy Thoughts'.

At the core of the philosophy of Tejgyan is the Power of Acceptance. Acceptance has profound meaning and is at the core of our Being. It is Acceptance that brings forth true love, joy and peace.

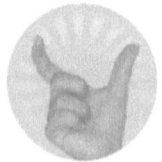

Symbol of Acceptance

The Symbol of Acceptance – shown above – is a representation of this truth. The symbol represents brackets. Whatever occurs in life falls within these brackets that signify acceptance of whatever is. Hence, this symbol forms the centerpiece of the Foundation's MaNaN Ashram.

The Foundation is creating a highly evolved society through:
- Tejgyan Programs (Retreats, YouTube Webcasts)
- Tejgyan Books and Apps
- Tejgyan Projects (Value education, Women empowerment, Peace initiatives)

The Foundation undertakes projects to elevate the level of consciousness among students, youth, women, senior citizens, teachers, doctors, leaders, professionals, corporate and Government organizations, police force, prisoners etc.

Now you can register online for
the following retreats

**Maha Aasmani
Param Gyan Shivir**
(5 Days Residential Retreat in Hindi)

Mini Maha Aasmani Shivir
3 Days (Residential) Retreat for Teens

🔍 www.tejgyan.org

Books can be delivered at your doorstep by registered post or courier. You can request the same through postal money order or pay by VPP. Please send the money order to either of the following two addresses:

WOW Publishings Pvt. Ltd.

1. Registered Office: E-4, Vaibhav Nagar, Near Tapovan Mandir, Pimpri, Pune - 411017.

2. Post Box No. 36, Pimpri Colony Post Office, Pimpri, Pune - 411017
Phone No: (+91) 9011013210 / 9623457873

You can also order your copy at the online store:
www.gethappythoughts.org

*Free Shipping plus 10% Discount on purchases above Rs. 500/-

For further details contact:
Tejgyan Global Foundation
Registered Office:
Happy Thoughts Building, Vikrant Complex, Near Tapovan Mandir, Pimpri, Pune 411017, Maharashtra, India.
Contact No: 020-27411240, 27412576
Email: mail@tejgyan.com

MaNaN Ashram:
Survey No. 43, Sanas Nagar, Nandoshi gaon, Kirkatwadi Phata, Sinhagad Road, Tal. Haveli, Dist. Pune 411024, Maharashtra, India.
Contact No: 992100 8060.

Hyderabad: 9885558100, **Bangalore:** 9880412588, **Delhi :** 9891059875, **Nashik:** 9326967980, **Mumbai:** 9373440985

For accessing our unique 'System for Wisdom' from self-help to self-realization, please follow us on:

	Website Online Shopping/ Blog	www.tejgyan.org www.gethappythoughts.org
	Video Channel	www.youtube.com/tejgyan For Q&A videos: http://goo.gl/YA81DQ
	Social networking	www.facebook.com/tejgyan
	Social networking	www.twitter.com/sirshree
	Internet Radio	http://www.tejgyan.org/internetradio.aspx

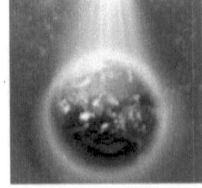

Pray for World Peace along with thousands of others every day at 09:09am and 09:09pm

Divine Light of Love, Bliss and Peace is Showering;
The Golden Light of Higher Consciousness is Rising;
All negativity on Earth is Dissolving;
Everyone is in Peace and Blissfully Shining;
O God, Gratitude for Everything!

www.ingramcontent.com/pod-product-compliance
Lightning Source LLC
LaVergne TN
LVHW040143080526
838202LV00042B/3011